Pony Express Route 1860-1861

MINNESOTA

NORTH DAKOTA

SOUTH DAKOTA

WYOMING

RAPID CITY

Missouri River

IOWA

Rock Creek Station

Horseshoe Station

NEBRASKA

SIOUX CITY

OMAHA

COUNCIL BLUFFS

Fort Laramie

LINCOLN

MISSOURI

ST. JOSEPH

DENVER

ABILENE

TOPEKA

COLORADO

KANSAS

stations •
trail —
forts ■
cities ⊙

TEXAS

OKLAHOMA

NEW MEXICO

JIMMY SPOON
—AND THE—
PONY EXPRESS

St. Joseph Pony Express riders: (clockwise from the top left) Billy Richardson, Johnny Fry, Charley Cliff, Gus Cliff. (Courtesy of Pony Express Museum, St. Joseph, MO)

JIMMY SPOON
—AND THE—
PONY EXPRESS

KRISTIANA GREGORY

SCHOLASTIC
HARDCOVER

Scholastic Inc.
New York

For information regarding permission, write to Scholastic Inc.,
555 Broadway, New York, New York 10012.

Library of Congress Cataloging-in-Publication Data
Gregory, Kristiana.
Jimmy Spoon and the Pony Express / Kristiana Gregory.
p.   cm.
Sequel to: The legend of Jimmy Spoon.
Summary: Having returned from living with his friends the
Shoshoni, seventeen-year-old Jimmy Spoon grows restless again and
seeks adventure by taking a job with the Pony Express.
ISBN 0–590–46577–5
[1. Pony express—Fiction. 2. Frontier and pioneer life—West
(U.S.)—Fiction.]   I. Title.
PZ7.G8619Ji   1994
[Fic]—dc20   93-47420
                                                        CIP
                                                        AC

12 11 10 9 8 7 6 5 4 3 2   5 6 7 8 9/9 0/0

Designed by Dawn Antoniello

Printed in the U.S.A.   37

First printing, October 1994

For my brother and sister, cherished friends from childhood and friends still:
Rob Gregory and Janet Gregory Coen,
and
to the memory of
Theron Dunn
Na? Dagwiship
1969–1993
A "Sho-Ban" Warrior taken too soon

CONTENTS

Contents

AUTHOR'S NOTE

Jimmy Spoon and the Pony Express continues the adventures from *The Legend of Jimmy Spoon*. Both novels are fiction based on the memoirs, *Among the Shoshones*, by Elijah Nicholas Wilson. The town of Wilson, Wyoming, named for that author, is at the southern base of the Grand Tetons in Wyoming.

In the 1850s, a letter mailed from New York took six to eight weeks to reach San Francisco: First it traveled by ship south to the Gulf of Mexico, then by mule and canoe across Panama, and again by ship up to California. If a letter went by covered wagon along the Overland Trail, it could take months. People joked that news had already been forgotten on the East Coast by the time folks on the West Coast heard it.

The Pony Express began April 3, 1860, covered a distance of nearly 2,000 miles, and lasted just eighteen months. News was telegraphed from various eastern cities to St. Joseph, Missouri, where someone in a tiny office would decode the clicking, then write the message on lightweight paper and slip it into an envelope. Postage was five dollars a half ounce. The telegram — along with military dispatches and newspapers printed on special tissue — was put into one of four padlocked pouches of the *mochila* (Spanish for knapsack).

Riders averaged ten miles an hour, racing relay-style all the way to Sacramento in just ten days. Theoretically a fresh horse would be waiting every fifteen miles, a fresh rider every fifty or so. Because there was a telegraph office in Carson City, Nevada, some news could be wired ahead to California with a message that the rest of the mail was on its way.

On October 24, 1861, the telegraph wire system was completed in Salt Lake City, Utah. Though rates were high — up to seventy-five cents a word — messages now could be sent cross-country in just four hours, making the Pony Express obsolete.

WANTED: Young, skinny, wiry fellows not over 18. Must be expert riders, willing to risk death daily, orphans preferred. Wages $25 a week . . .

—March 1860 newspaper ad

"A whiz and a hail, and the swift phantom of the desert was gone before we could get our heads out of the windows."

—Author Mark Twain,
on sighting a Pony Express
rider from his stagecoach,
summer 1861

JIMMY SPOON
—AND THE—
PONY EXPRESS

1

ORPHANS PREFERRED

Winter sunlight slanted in through the broad windows of Spoon's Fancy Store. Jimmy gazed longingly outside at the wagons rattling along the muddy road and the men on horseback, all going someplace in the crisp fresh air. He leaned over the glass countertop where his reflection showed his bow tie was crooked again. His sandy brown hair curled above his collar, which was so stiff with starch, it scraped his neck miserably. The start of a moustache on his upper lip was the only good thing about this week.

What bothered him more than being cooped up in his father's store were the female customers warming themselves around the small iron stove.

They were his sisters' friends and they were whispering about him.

"When I get married," one of them boldly announced, "I'm going to shop here for my *trousseau*, at Salt Lake City's finest fancy store." Jimmy blushed when he heard the word *trousseau*, knowing it meant items a bride wears on her honeymoon. He looked helplessly out the window, aware that the girls watched him adoringly.

How he ached to be in the fresh air, away from the city. Instead of suffering in this store, he wished that he could be with his Shoshoni friends, hunting elk or walking in the woods with Nahanee, lovely Nahanee.

Jimmy's eyes fell on a newspaper his father had left on the counter. A headline on the front page made him catch his breath. As he picked it up, his heart began to race with excitement.

"Boy howdy!" he yelled, his voice echoing off the tall ceilings.

The girls looked up, surprised. Jimmy was usually so shy around them, he either blushed or stuttered. Never had they heard him holler.

Thinking he should explain himself, Jimmy read out loud the news that would surely captivate them: "WANTED: Young, skinny, wiry fellows not over 18. Must be expert riders, willing to risk death daily, orphans preferred. Wages $25 a week. . . .

"That's me all right!" he said. "It's for mail delivery, from St. Joe all the way to Sacramento in just ten days — ten days! — instead of six weeks. This is good news — what am I saying? — this is the *best* news, a job away from home!'' Jimmy burst out with a giddy laugh, then stopped himself when he saw the girls' startled faces. How would he be able to contain himself until the store closed, another six hours away?

Lillian Zimmerman's dress rustled as she moved down the aisles toward him. Her shoes clicked daintily on the clean wood floor. She and Jimmy had known each other since childhood. If anyone would understand the reason for his new happiness, it was Lillian.

When she put her slender hands on the counter, Jimmy caught a scent of her perfume and was surprised how good it made him feel.

He felt his face get warm. ''Hello, Lillian.''

''Hello.'' She smiled at him shyly, then whispered, ''Jimmy, I thought you wanted to be a captain in the army like my father.''

''I do. I mean, I did. Maybe I'll do both.''

''Well then, you'd better learn to dress properly. Your shirt is inside out again.''

It was snowing when Jimmy hung the CLOSED sign in the window. He stepped outside, then, with the bell tinkling against the door, shut and locked it. The mud was frozen now and powdery white. A carriage with a tin lantern swinging by the seat passed quickly behind a trotting mare.

Jimmy couldn't wait to find his friends, the Cone brothers and Pen Hailey. He hurried along the planked sidewalk, his coat pulled above his ears for warmth. As he rounded the corner by the

3

houses where Brigham Young lived with his many wives, children, and hired help, Jimmy heard shouts. Three boys burst through a gate in the high stone wall that surrounded the estate.

"Jimmy!"

"Fellas!" Jimmy swatted them playfully with the *Deseret News*.

"Can you believe it, Jim, a pony express? Know what that means? Folks'll be so happy to get their mail in ten days, the riders could end up heroes."

Heroes. Now this was something Jimmy hadn't considered, but the idea appealed to him very much. Something bothered him, though.

"I'm not an orphan," he said, as if he'd just realized this.

"That's true, Jim, but I am. So's Will here and Nick. We're orphans, sure, but ain't nobody can ride a horse good as you, Jimmy. Nobody."

"Maybe . . . maybe not. Another thing, Pa needs my help to run the store and now that I think of it Mother would never consent. . . ." Jimmy looked down. He was remembering how he'd run away from home when he was twelve and for two happy years lived with the Shoshoni Indians. When he finally returned to his mother, she was so happy to see him she had wept with joy.

Jimmy had promised her he would never again run away.

Snowflakes hissed as they drifted onto the boys' hair and thin shoulders. Their breath made steam in the cold air. The ten eastern gables of the Lion House were beginning to glow with candlelight.

Downstairs in the Beehive House there was a silhouette of someone carrying firewood to the hearth. From one of the kitchens on the estate, an aroma of cooking meat drifted out an open window.

Nick and Will, who were hungry and who were not wearing coats, began rubbing their arms for warmth. Their woolen shirts felt thinner by the moment. The cold and the delicious smell of supper made the boys look at one another, trying quickly to think of some way to convince Jimmy to change his mind.

"Tryouts are tomorrow, Jim," Pen said, knowing how much Jimmy enjoyed showing off. "One of the trail bosses from Russell, Majors & Waddell is comin' in with some wild mustangs. Y'gotta come with us, Jimmy. Pay's good. It's the same we're getting from President Young but alls we do is clean out stables, pigeon coops 'n' such that puts a boy to sleep. Pony Express riders won't be bored and they sure won't be slaves, that's my guess."

Will began stomping his cold feet and rubbing his arms faster. "Practically the whole town of Salt Lake'll be watching," he said. "They're turning Main Street into a rodeo arena come noon, snow or no snow, what d'you say?"

Jimmy's mind raced. Leaving home for a job, now that was different from running away. Surely his mother would understand. He had worked faithfully for his father for almost three years and he now had a younger brother: Little Thomas could be the one to take over the store someday.

The idea of again living in the wilderness thrilled Jimmy. He might be able to see some of his Shoshoni brothers, or at least he would feel closer to them knowing their trails were nearby. Also, there would be danger and Jimmy would be a hero. Who could resist that? He had another thought: The rodeo would be a chance to show Lillian Zimmerman that on a horse he could wear his shirt any way he darned pleased.

"Fellas," Jimmy said, giving each shivering boy a hearty handshake, "noon sounds so good t'me, I'll be there at eleven!"

2

RODEO

Piles of shoveled snow were on the shady side of Main Street where women in wool capes and bonnets began to gather. In the growing excitement, children chased each other, some swung from the damp hitching rails, other played hide-and-seek behind their mothers' skirts.

Most of the men made themselves appear important by inspecting the corral of wagons that now formed an arena in the wide street. They inspected ropes, they inspected — from a safe distance — the huffing, pawing mustangs that paced in an outer corral.

When Mr. Alexander Majors stood on a wagon seat, the crowd fell silent. He wore a stovepipe hat and long dress coat, and his beard was freshly barbered.

"Ladies and gentlemen," he yelled with raised arms. "This is not for the fainthearted nor the pale in spirit. We have wild horses and we have boys who want to ride 'em. Come April *some* of these boys will be racing across the Territory where unsavory thugs and outlaws wait in ambush, folks, where hostile Indians are looking for scalps.

"But *I'm* looking for heroes today, ladies and gentlemen, heroes who'll help deliver mail between the east and west coasts faster than ever before. Now let's see what these boys can do!"

The crowd roared with enthusiasm. The boys waiting by the horses threw hats in the air and congratulated one another as if they were already galloping across the desert. Out of nearly sixty confident boys that noon, just twenty-three would stay in the saddle long enough to buck around the ring. Only eleven of them would be hired by Russell, Majors & Waddell to be Pony Express riders on the most rugged and dangerous route of all: Salt Lake City to Reno and back.

As wranglers boosted each contestant into the saddle before opening the chute, they wondered if these boys realized what they might be getting into. There were twelve-year-olds half as tall as the horse, thin boys lighter than their sisters, boys who'd never ridden anything except a bumpy plow seat. One by one they slid off, were bucked off, or chickened out at the last minute.

By two o'clock, the Cone brothers had each

8

made it three times around and each survived a furiously bucking stallion. Pen Hailey made it twice with a safe leap out of the saddle. Jimmy sat on a post by the corral, calmly waiting for his turn. He was pleased to see a cluster of girls watching him from the second-floor porch of his father's store. There was no mistaking his twin sister Nan in her blue cloak and next to her Lillian Zimmerman, red-cheeked from the frosty air.

His parents were also watching with his other sisters and little brother. They waved and called Jimmy's name every time he looked up. The atmosphere was that of a holiday as most businesses had closed. The fire brigade's band played patriotic marches and Mr. Diggle put his popcorn wagon to work, filling the air with the luscious aroma of hot buttery corn.

The night before, when Jimmy had talked to his family about the newspaper article, his father's eyes lit up. With a dreamy look he exclaimed, "By Jove, son! If I were your age, I'd do it! Why, the very future of our country depends on young patriots like you." Jimmy's mother had stood quietly near the stove. He knew by her face that there were things he needed to think through, things he needed to tell her.

"James Henry Spoon!" called the voice of Mr. Majors.

Jimmy looked up. It was his turn. "Sir!" he answered. Knowing that everyone's eyes were upon him, he straightened his shoulders and, feeling a nervous twist in his stomach, took a deep breath.

He made a handsome sight. His pants were tucked into tall leather boots and he wore the red flannel shirt his mother had made him. Few knew that the bandana tied around his neck had been a farewell gift from Chief Washakie, or that a pocket inside Jimmy's vest held an eagle feather. He took another deep breath, drawing strength from the memory of how he'd earned the eagle feather. He also remembered the river where Washakie taught him to ride his first wild pony. What a happy day that had been.

The mustang stomped in its chute, enraged to be confined. Its nostrils flared when Jimmy approached, its ears lay back. The crowd grew still.

"Easy, fella," Jimmy said softly as he climbed the fence. "I'm not gonna hurt you. Easy." He reached under its belly to uncinch the saddle. It dropped to the mud. Gently he stroked behind its fuzzy ear, slipping his fingers under the harness, unbuckling it, then pulling it down over the nose so the bit could come out. Now the horse was as bare as when captured on the prairie. Jimmy nodded to the wrangler to open the gate.

"Son, you ain't on the horse, yet."

"I will be soon enough. Now kindly open it."

The wrangler hesitated. He had never seen anyone ride these horses bareback except Indians. What if the boy got hurt?

"Please, mister."

"You're the boss, sonny." He flung open the gate, freeing the powerful animal. As it bolted from the chute, Jimmy launched himself from the fence as if diving across a pond. When he landed safely on its back, a cry of relief rose from the spectators.

Jimmy laced his fingers into the tangled mane, squeezed his legs against its sides, and began leading the horse in a graceful canter around the ring. On the second loop, Jimmy slid down against its side, still holding on with his strong legs, making it appear that there was no rider. He thrust his arm under the horse's neck, pretending to fire an arrow, a trick he had learned from Nampa and the other warriors. A man tall in the saddle makes an easy target, they had taught him. This memory made Jimmy wish he were riding through a meadow and that the cheering crowd was instead his beloved Shoshoni.

As the horse neared Mr. Majors, Jimmy pulled himself up, tucked one foot under himself in a crouch, then leapt up to the wagon. With a smile, Jimmy saluted the astonished man, and jumped down. He sprinted across the arena where he caught up to the horse, grabbed its mane, then sprung up as easily as if there had been stirrups.

Pen Hailey slapped Jimmy's back in congratulations as Jimmy scraped manure from his boots on the edge of the planked sidewalk. Mr. Majors hurried over and, extending his right hand, grinned like an uncle. "Name's Alexander Majors. Where'd you learn to handle a horse like that, son?"

Before Jimmy could answer, his younger sisters and his brother broke through the crowd. The four-year-old boy holding Lucy's hand gazed up at Mr.

Majors from under his tweed cap. "Jimmy killed a bear once," Thomas said.

Annie pulled the man's sleeve, knowing he was the one in charge. "Jimmy's brave," she assured him. "He rode clear up to Fort Hall with no pants on, just his shirt and his bare behind. We saw!"

"Liar," said Emma, sticking her tongue out at her sister, then turning to Mr. Majors all polite. "He's the bravest boy there is, sir. He's Chief Washkey's blood brother, just ask Pa, and he speaks Sho-sho-nee as good as English."

Mr. Majors was amused by the children's reports. At the mention of the chief's name he grew thoughtful. He took off his hat and seemed to study it. "Now *there* is a man I hold in high esteem, Washakie, a man of peace. We met several years ago at Fort Hall."

Jimmy felt his throat tighten. He was proud to be Washakie's adopted brother. Hearing a stranger speak fondly of the chief made Jimmy realize how deeply he missed him.

"Sir?" he said, swallowing hard to keep his voice from breaking.

"Yes?"

"Did I get the job?"

Mr. Majors threw his head back in laughter, then reached out to shake Jimmy's hand again. "Forgive my poor manners, son. You had the job almost the moment I laid eyes on you."

3

NO CUSSING ALLOWED

By March, eighty boys, most of them under the age of nineteen, had been hired from several cities. Stations with corrals were being built every fifteen miles between St. Joseph, Missouri, and Sacramento, California. Jimmy, Pen, and the Cone brothers were assigned to the Ruby Valley Station in the Nevada desert. From there they would ride relays in either direction. Many of their resting spots would be just crude lean-tos with clearings in the dirt for them to sleep.

The morning before they were to leave, Jimmy found his mother hanging laundry on the line out back. When she saw he wanted to talk, she removed the wooden clothespin from her mouth and touched his hair in the affectionate gesture mothers have for their sons.

"Ma, I know you don't want me to go."

"True," she said. "Guess I'm afraid you'll not come back to us, Jimmy. I already missed out on some of your growin' up."

"Yes, ma'am."

"But your pa's right. You're seventeen, nearly a man. Why, someday you'll marry and be away from us anyhow." Mrs. Spoon gazed toward the towering Wasatch Mountains whose snowy ridges looked close enough to touch. The profile of her face seemed pretty to Jimmy, even though it showed the weariness of a woman who has borne eleven children. He wanted to throw himself into her comforting arms.

"I've been thinking on that, too, Ma. Mr. Majors says I'll be riding across Shoshoni trails. Washakie will be near, so will Nampa and Ga-mu. Maybe Old Mother will be traveling with them, too . . . I miss her, Ma."

Tears came to Mrs. Spoon's eyes, but she smiled. "Jimmy," she said with a sigh, "every day I thank our good Lord for Old Mother taking care of you those years, for loving you in my absence. I'm pleased you honor her."

Jimmy looked at the puddle by the well. Six ducklings splashed their wings for a bath, peeping loudly. He wished he could feel as lighthearted. "Mother, there's something else."

She looked at him. "Nahanee?"

Yes, he nodded. Words failed him now. Nearly

three years had passed since he'd seen Nahanee, but the image of that last morning kept returning to him, when the sunlight had caught the sheen of her hair, the beauty of her face. And how proudly she wore his bearclaw necklace.

Jimmy was sad to leave her. He hadn't wanted to return to his white family, but rumors of war made him think he must. Each week that had passed, he thought of her, though the memories were beginning to fade. Now for some reason, the pleasant scent of Lillian Zimmerman's perfume confused Jimmy. He longed for something he didn't understand, and this longing made him anxious to see his Indian family again.

Mrs. Spoon tenderly drew Jimmy to her, then held his shoulders. She could see the faint shadow of his mustache and how his jaw was looking more and more like his father's. The world of men and danger and heroes was not something she easily grasped. But she did understand matters of the heart.

"You'll do us proud, son, of that I'm certain." She looked again to the mountains. "Nahanee is a lucky young woman. I hope you find her, Jimmy."

After supper that evening, crowds swelled into the meeting hall to watch eleven boys be sworn in as Pony Express riders. Mormon President Brigham Young took the podium for a rousing speech. Laughter rippled through the audience as three yellow cats followed him onto the stage. They weaved between his legs and arched their backs against the tops of his boots. President Young was fond of cats and often kept scraps of dried fish in his pockets for them.

Jimmy's voice was clear and strong when he read the contract: "I hereby swear before the great and living God that while I am in the employ of Alexander Majors, I agree not to use profane language, not to get drunk, not to gamble, not to treat animals cruelly, and not to do anything else that is incompatible of the conduct of a gentleman.

"And I agree, if I violate any of the above conditions, to accept my discharge without any pay for my services." Jimmy signed the document, promising to work for one year. He then shook hands with Brigham Young, whose imposing figure and deep voice made Jimmy feel shy. He had known the president all his life because Mr. Spoon and Brigham Young were well acquainted.

Alexander Majors presented each boy with a palm-sized Bible, bound in suede. He held up his arms as if giving a benediction.

"Gentlemen," he said, "may you read these Holy precepts, treasure them in your hearts, and may they enrich your life and, as a result, enrich the lives of those around you. God bless you all. Wagons move out tomorrow. See you at sunrise!"

4

A NEW HOME

Jimmy stooped to enter the peculiar hut. It was a log cabin, but the logs were standing up like posts. Instead of windows each wall had a hole the size of a cookie, through which a rifle could point. Slivers of sunlight entered the dark room between the logs.

As Jimmy's eyes adjusted to the dim light, he saw eight bunks, a table, and north and south fireplaces. In one, a tall black coffeepot rattled over coals, and in the other was a cauldron of steamy water. The dirt floor was damp.

"Welcome to your home station, fellas," said the large man in the doorway. "Got a few weeks thereabouts before the Express starts and plenty t'do in between. Hole for outhouse gots to be dug, then

17

stable spiffed up. Your ponies'll be herded here any day now. Milo Young's the name, by the way, no relation to that pole-igamist Brigham Young. Supper's at sundown."

He hefted a juniper log that had been delivered by the wagon, then carried it on his shoulder toward a half-finished shed. Jimmy stepped outside where Pen and the Cone brothers were looking wide-eyed around them.

"Jimmy, we're plumb in the middle of nowheres," said Nick, his voice high with disappointment. He was fifteen, two years younger than his brother and Jimmy. Without speaking, they surveyed their new home.

Desert spread in every direction, interrupted by an occasional butte or low mountain range now purple in the waning sunlight. Sagebrush cast long round shadows. A plume of dust in the distance was the only sign wagons were continuing west with supplies and riders. The clink of a hammer echoed in the still air. In a corral beyond the shed a white-haired man named Mr. Tagg was nailing together a trough under the watchful eye of two gray mules.

"Well, boys," Jimmy said, picking up his bedroll and saddle, "let's make ourselves to home."

Mr. Tagg dished up stew. The crumbs in his beard meant they were having cornbread again tonight and that he'd already sampled plenty of it. He and Milo were the station keepers and while they were

18

hard workers and satisfactory cooks, Jimmy noted that neither had taken a bath or combed his oily hair in the two weeks they'd all been under the same roof. And it wasn't for lack of water. Ruby Lake was just two miles away.

Jimmy also had learned there was a spring ninety yards north of the cabin, which explained why the floor was damp. How pleased he and the boys were to find this small oasis, shaded by cottonwoods. There was a pool, chest deep, with a clean sandy bottom and enough room for one man to float on his back. The spring was surrounded by boulders with one narrow path to carry out buckets of water for the stock.

By the cabin door a long-handled dipper hung above a barrel. Jimmy took a drink, passed it to Will, then squinted toward the shimmery horizon. Blurred images, dark blue on brown, soon became soldiers on horseback. Dust billowed from their midst like summer clouds.

When Captain Zimmerman reined to a stop, Mr. Tagg took his horse. Jimmy listened to the soldiers. The words "injun" and "murder" were spat out. An Overland Stage had been attacked by Paiutes yesterday, March 22. The horses were stolen and Henry Harper, the driver, was scalped. This happened near Deep Creek, just half-a-day's ride away. A sick feeling made Jimmy want to sit down.

"What's the matter, Jim?" Pen asked, joining him cross-legged in the dirt.

"Don't feel s'good, somehow."

"Are you scared?"

Jimmy shook his head, thinking. "Nope, I'm not scared, Pen."

The boys watched Captain Zimmerman fill his canteen by dunking it into the barrel. Bubbles rose to the dark surface. The dozen men from the Fourth Cavalry were adjusting saddles and scooping hats into the troughs to douse their heads; some rolled cigarettes or faced away to relieve themselves.

"We'll be all right, Jim, you'll see," Pen said, hoping to comfort his friend. Pen's curly blond hair was windblown and dusty. His face was sunburned, and even his freckles were pink. This was because his hat was too big and kept blowing off. For boys working in the desert, there was no shade except under a hat.

"We're trespassers," Jimmy said to Pen some moments later.

"What d'you mean?"

"That's why Paiutes are mad enough to kill." Jimmy remembered Washakie's words, how the *tybos*, white people, were moving in uninvited. How fences were blocking trails, how wagon wheels were crushing the precious camas flower. Without the flower, there would be no roots to eat, Jimmy explained.

Pen considered this. "If Indians don't want us riding through their land . . . Jim, are they really going to try to kill us? Mr. Majors said so, but I didn't believe him."

Jimmy didn't answer. He was furious at himself. *How could he have so recklessly signed up to be a tres-*

passer? He'd only been thinking of himself, how he wanted to be a hero and show Lillian Zimmerman a thing or two. He wanted to see Old Mother again and to find Nahanee. These were things *he* wanted.

He hadn't considered what the Shoshoni might think of *Dawii*, Young Brother to the chief, helping to make the country one big safe place for *tybos*. The sick feeling inside Jimmy deepened to shame. It was too late for him to back out. He'd signed a contract, taken an oath. He had promised to help see the mail through.

5

FAST AS THE WIND

Jimmy woke suddenly. Embers in the fireplaces were the only light in the small cabin. He lay in his bunk, listening. In the very far distance, a rider was approaching.

It was two o'clock in the morning, April 6, 1860. Three days earlier, a boy in Missouri and a boy in California began galloping full speed toward each other. Every fifteen miles a fresh horse would be waiting, and every fifty or so miles, a fresh rider. Somewhere in the vast Nevada desert, two boys would pass each other so swiftly, there'd be no time to even shout "hello."

This thought made Jimmy bolt upright and hurriedly pull on his pants. *Could this be the rider he was to relieve? So soon?*

Blankets were thrown back and bare feet struggled into cold, stiff boots: A rider was coming! Mr. Tagg and Will rushed outside to ready a horse, and Pen tried to boost Jimmy's courage.

"You're the best there is, Jim. No Pie-oot will catch *you*, guaranteed."

Milo poured steaming coffee into a tin cup and handed it to Jimmy with a chunk of bread.

"Mornin', son," he said, bending close. His breath stunk from an infected tooth, but Jimmy didn't mind. Despite Milo's unwashed body and unpleasant odors, he was as kind as an old grandfather. "We're countin' on you, Jim. Soon's you reach Roberts Crik Station, ride the next relay back. Mr. Tagg'll keep the coffee on, just like always."

"Thanks, Milo. I'll try my best." Jimmy drank the scalding liquid, but tucked the bread inside his shirt. He was too nervous to eat. He lifted his coat off a peg in the wall and stepped out into the cold night.

Silhouetted against the starry horizon was a small, moving shape. It rose and fell, again and again. The faint rumbling Jimmy had heard earlier was now clearly the sound of hoofbeats. A knot clenched in his stomach, a mixture of fear and excitement. He prayed Washakie would understand he had a job to do.

Jimmy was grateful for the full moon rising in the east because it illuminated the trail like a silver ribbon. *Had Mr. Majors planned it this way, so the first riders would be guided by moonlight?*

Before he could think further, the rider, a boy

named Charlie Cliff, was in front of the cabin, leaping off his foaming horse. Charlie lifted the *mochila*, which was a wafer-thin square of leather with four pockets, off the saddle, and tossed it to Mr. Tagg yelling, "Trail's clear!" This meant there were no Indians chasing him.

Jimmy's horse was rearing with impatience as Mr. Tagg slipped the *mochila* over the horn of its saddle. Nick held the halter while Jimmy swung up. Before his right boot could fit into the stirrup, the horse bolted forward and he was on his way, galloping westward across the cold night desert.

Through the thundering of hooves a wisp of a voice reached him. "Godspeed, Jimmy!" called Milo.

Jimmy's horse sped on. Moonlight behind them made it appear they were chasing their shadow. After an hour his sides ached and he was thirsty. Jimmy was relieved when ahead there appeared the dark shape of a hut. Men were leading a horse from a corral. Maybe the two minutes allowed for changing mounts would be enough for Jimmy to catch his breath.

After jumping down, he transferred the *mochila* to the fresh animal. An eager boy about nine years old pressed a cup of water into his hand.

"What's it like, Mister?" the boy asked.

Jimmy took a drink. "Trail's clear," he responded in his deepest voice. He mounted, then, smiling down at the youngster, slapped the reins against the horse's flank.

"Yee-up!" he yelled. No one saw Jimmy's grin, or knew that his heart soared with happiness. A small boy had called him "Mister" and had pulled a souvenir strand from his pony's tail.

Yes, sir, this was his kind of job.

6

TROUBLE

Roberts Creek Station was about sixty miles west of Ruby Valley. It looked like a ranch to Jimmy. A blacksmith was shoeing a mule, and several soldiers sat nearby cleaning their rifles. They all watched Jimmy admiringly as he tossed the *mochila* then walked his exhausted horse to the corral.

The hostel was spacious inside, with wide plank floors and windows with curtains. Three long tables were heavy with breakfast and the elbows of overland travelers. Voices were loud and animated. Jimmy slumped onto one of the benches, too tired to remove his boots, but not too tired to smile at those around him. He was proud that so many people waved to him and shouted, "Howdy, boy!"

On the floor next to him was a wooden box with

a blanket and a sleeping baby inside. The baby had round pink cheeks and it did not seem to be bothered by the noise.

Jimmy tasted dried blood on his lips and felt with his tongue how parched his mouth was. Riding fast for five hours, even though he changed horses three times, was harder than he had thought it would be. His legs ached and he knew they were raw in places. Remembering the bread Milo had given him, he reached into his shirt, but sweat had made the bread soggy.

A woman with strong, tanned arms set a steaming bowl of oatmeal in front of Jimmy. Butter pooled in its center, melting into clumps of brown sugar.

"You look wore out," she said to him. "I'm Mrs. Roberts and that there's baby Lucy. Me and Tom run Roberts Crik and we're proud to have you boys stoppen here. Meals are on the house." From the center of the table she took someone's plate of half-eaten bread and gave it to Jimmy. Then, searching among the other diners, she found a mug of unfinished milk. There were bits of chewed food floating on top, but Jimmy was so thirsty he drank it straight down.

He didn't remember being led to the bunkhouse or even stretching out. But someone was now shaking his shoulder, waking him from a deep sleep. In another instant he was on a horse, still groggy, but carrying the mail east under a blue, cloudless sky, the warm afternoon sun at his back.

This is the life, he thought. Cheers from stagecoach passengers rang pleasantly in his ears. Folks liked him, he was important. What he had failed to notice, however, was that the rider he replaced was pale with fright and had been unable to speak. Nor had Jimmy noticed that soldiers were forming ranks beyond the corral.

When Jimmy sighted Sulphur Creek, he was just coming around a bluff and out of a dry riverbed. Wind blew the fine alkali dust into his eyes and mouth. Its salty taste made him even more thirsty. Jimmy was glad a fresh horse would be waiting because this one was beginning to tire. It seemed odd though, that the corral was empty with no one to greet him.

"Hello?" Jimmy called. Cautiously he dismounted, looping the reins around a post. His horse drank from a large bucket of water, and Jimmy cupped a drink for himself. "Hello?" he called again.

The sudden force of someone grabbing him knocked Jimmy to the ground, but it was only a small boy whose tear-stained face pleaded silently with him.

"Whoa . . . what happened, fella? Where's your pa?"

Still clinging to him, the boy led Jimmy inside. A man sat against the hearth shivering in pain. The long shaft of an arrow protruded from his thigh. His eyes were glazed. When he saw Jimmy he tried to speak, but his voice was hoarse.

"Pie-oots," he whispered.

Jimmy noticed a figure cowering in the corner,

someone he recognized as a fellow rider. But this boy rocked back and forth, whimpering.

"I quit, I plain quit," he sobbed. "They killed Uncle, they just outright kilt 'im.'"

Jimmy forced himself to think. *What was he to do?* Gently prying the boy's small arms off his, he set him on a bunk and tucked a blanket around him, then hurried outside. He was shocked to see a dead man sprawled in a trough, red water seeping into the dirt. Tracks showed that one group of Indians headed north with the stolen horses. With increasing alarm, Jimmy circled the corral.

Nine, possibly twelve, Paiutes were riding east toward Ruby Valley. Toward his home station. He knelt down to feel the droppings. They were still warm. Jimmy knew this group was not too far away.

If he hurried, he might be able to skirt their trail and ride the fifteen miles to Ruby Valley in time to warn Milo and Mr. Tagg. *But what about the soldiers at Roberts Creek? Should he turn back and notify them instead?* It would be getting dark soon and the moon wouldn't be rising for several hours.

Jimmy raced back to the cabin. "This is gonna hurt," he said to the station keeper, kneeling beside him. "But it'll be quick. We gotta do it so's you don't lose your leg."

Before the man could protest, Jimmy had snapped the shaft in two and pushed the end with the arrowhead through the back of the thigh. The man's eyes rolled up and he groaned in agony.

Jimmy found a tin of salt. He pinched enough

to pack into the bleeding wound, then grabbed a small rag rug from the hearth. He wrapped it around the injured leg.

"Hold it tight till the blood stops," he instructed. Then turning to the littlest boy, he smiled. "Your pa's gonna be all right, sonny. Help's on the way."

In the instant that Jimmy swung onto his horse he decided not to return to Roberts Creek. He must warn his friends. But this made Jimmy feel sad inside. He had such understanding and love for Indian people, how could he possibly fight them?

7

A Lonely Birthday

Jimmy could see that the Paiutes heading east had ridden around the north side of a butte. He galloped south, through a sandy arroyo, then up onto a trail that looked like a long piece of string stretching through the sagebrush.

Soon enough he saw the dust of many horses to his left, their riders hidden by the powdery alkali that rose from the trail. Jimmy could tell he was gaining on them even though his path was rough with weeds and burrows.

By the time the Indians saw Jimmy, he had passed them and made it through Shadow Canyon. Now he was closing in on Ruby Valley Station, the *mochila* still safe underneath him. He felt sorry to be pushing his horse so hard. Most of all, he was sorry these Indians believed he was an enemy.

With the setting sun at his back, Jimmy's shadow spilled in front of him like a long stain. He looked over his shoulder and was surprised to see the dust moving north. Perhaps it was the approaching darkness that turned his pursuers homeward or perhaps they knew soldiers were close.

An hour-and-a-half after leaving Sulphur Creek, he saw the cabin and Milo leading a relief horse from the corral. Moments later, Jimmy dismounted and tossed over the *mochila*. He wished he were the one continuing to Salt Lake City instead of young Nick Cone.

On the warm afternoon of May 7, Captain Zimmerman rode in with bad news. While his soldiers watered their horses he cussed about the Indians.

"Bad enough about Sulphur Creek, but now Williams Station there on Carson River, it was burned to the ground," he reported. His sunburned face looked angry. "Oscar and David Williams were kilt, along with three of their men. Cold Springs Station, sure it's two hundred miles from here, but it's still our front yard 'far as I'm concerned — it was burned, too, the boss and his stable boys scalped. Those savages are dangerous, worse 'n hornets stirred up."

The Captain's saddle creaked as he stepped into the stirrup and pulled himself up. His dark blue uniform was dusty. He swigged from his canteen, then, with water dripping from his chin, yelled for all to hear.

"Until further notice, Pony riders are to stay put, no relays. Got to rebuild stations and bring in more horses, more men. The army'll escort an Overland Stage now 'n' then, but otherwise, trail's closed. Shut down!"

Jimmy was worried. "Sir," he said, shading his eyes to look up. "What if Paiutes come after *us*? What'll we do?"

"Sonny, you can shine your shoes if you want. But me, I'd keep those guns loaded and an eye wide-open. Good day!" With a crisp salute he cantered toward the corral where his soldiers were mounting.

Marks chiseled in the wall told Jimmy it was May 13, his birthday. He looked around the cluttered room at the messy beds and plates of yesterday's food. A rustle among the sacks of flour and potatoes meant desert rats had moved in and were helping themselves.

Things were not turning out the way he had planned. One week had passed since his last ride and the trail was still closed. His father's store would be more interesting than this lonely way station. He didn't like being afraid of Indians or that they were considered enemies. He didn't like how Captain Zimmerman had said to *shoot first, ask questions later*. What would Washakie think of Dawii, taking orders from such a man?

These things confused Jimmy and filled him with doubts: Maybe he shouldn't try to find his Shoshoni friends, maybe he had let too much time pass and they'd forgotten him. Or maybe they no longer cared.

Jimmy felt sad. He peered out the low doorway where he could see Will and Mr. Tagg riding the perimeter in the hot sun. Flowering sagebrush made the desert look golden and, in the sky, clouds plumed like towers of cotton. It was a lovely, peaceful day, which made Jimmy yearn for the excitement of the trail, something to perk him up.

No one at Ruby Valley knew it was his birthday, so there would be no cake or presents. Jimmy felt comforted knowing his parents were thinking of him, and when he realized he was now eighteen years old, he felt even better.

"This calls for a swim, that's what!"

At the spring he peeled off his shirt and trousers. He dunked them a few times, wrung them out, then draped them over boulders to dry.

While he floated on his back he watched clouds drift across the turquoise sky. A red-tailed hawk circled overhead in the still air, diving from Jimmy's sight, then rising again with a small furry creature in its talons.

For a moment he forgot about being lonesome. A pleasant memory made him smile. It had been a warm day like this. Along the river, tipis stood in the shade of cottonwood trees, and cooking fires filled the air with wood smoke. Jimmy had been chasing another boy above the waterfall when he saw below him a pool, deep and crystal clear.

Nahanee was bathing with her friends.

He knew he shouldn't watch, but he couldn't help himself. She was beautiful, the graceful way she braided her wet hair.

He was surprised this memory made him ache. For days now he had watched the wide sky and listened as wind rustled the desert grass. He'd sat so still for so long a yellow-backed spiny lizard had taken a nap on the toe of his boot. Jimmy gazed at the northern trails, hoping to see some of his old friends on a hunt or gathering camas roots, but the trails were empty. Perhaps it was no longer safe for them to come this far south.

Jimmy missed the way of the Shoshoni. He yearned to be with Nahanee, to laugh with her again and watch eagles nesting.

If she and the others would not be traveling to Ruby Valley, should Jimmy try to look for them anyway? Could he bear to know they might have forgotten him?

8

OUTLAWS

Day by day the desert began heating up, like a skillet on a low, steady flame. The thermometer nailed outside on the shady north wall rose above ninety degrees each noon. Wild sunflowers bloomed on the sod roof, making the cabin look as if it wore a fuzzy gold hat.

By mid-June Captain Zimmerman declared the trails passable for mail and travelers. "Not as dangerous," were his words. He did not say the trails were safe.

White-topped wagons drawn by mules and oxen once again lumbered through Ruby Valley on their long journey west. Emigrants cheered upon sighting the dust of an Express rider. For an exhilarating moment they could see the small, crouched boy on his pony, but he passed so swiftly he was gone in a blink.

It was a warm, still afternoon when Jack Slade cantered in from Deep Creek. He was one of the few riders who was older than Jimmy. For some odd reason Slade had no *mochila* and he was in no hurry.

"Salutations, gentlemen," he said pleasantly as he dismounted. "I feel duty bound to warn you that Rex Dooley and his gang are on the loose again. Till the posse catches up with them, you best stay clear of Eagle Canyon. They caused a lot of trouble for some miners thereabouts."

"What sort of trouble?" asked Mr. Tagg.

"Well, to be perfectly frank, gentlemen . . . the miners are dead."

"Is that so?" Milo exchanged knowing looks with Mr. Tagg.

"That's right," Slade answered. "Now if you'll excuse me, I must continue on my journey. I've been reassigned to Carson City Station." He filled his canteen, then, while his horse drank from the barrel, he freshened up. He ran a comb through his shoulder-length hair and meticulously brushed the dust off his sleeves. By the time he straightened his black string tie and repositioned his hat, he looked ready to dance in a saloon, not ride miles under a hot sun.

Jimmy admired Slade's gun and how his holster creaked when he moved. He wished he and the other boys could carry a six-shooter, but the weight was too much for a speeding pony; they were even told not to ride with a pocketknife.

"Well, don't worry about us, Jack," Jimmy said with confidence, even though he'd never met the outlaws. "We'll keep a lookout. Rex Dooley can't touch us. He's a baby. Far as *I'm* concerned, he's still in diapers."

The man laughed. "Those Dooley boys would hang a fool like you and enjoy it more than a birthday party. Diapers, that's good!"

Still laughing, he pulled himself up into his saddle and, without a word, whipped his horse into a gallop. In a moment he was gone.

Milo tipped his hat over his eyes and squinted toward the trail. He shook his head.

"Is anything wrong?" Jimmy asked.

"Jim," Milo said, resting a grandfatherly hand on his shoulder. "Mr. Tagg and I worked with Slade in the stockyards back in Missour-a. We were shocked when he was hired to ride for the Pony Express. Few folks realize that Jack Slade is a cold-blooded killer."

"A *killer*?"

"Twenty-two dead far as we know, and one crippled — got his leg shot off almost," said Mr. Tagg.

Jimmy's eyes grew wide. "You mean he's killed twenty-two people?"

"Yes, sir. Even cut off the ears of one fella and carried 'em around for souvenirs, mementos. Jim, if I ain't mistaken, that's Pen Hailey coming over the rise and you're next rider up."

9

RUNAWAY STAGE

As Jimmy sped westward he tried to imagine what a pair of cutoff ears would look like. Did Jack Slade keep the ears in his pocket or in a nice little case with velvet lining? Surely there would be blood and a sickening smell, much like the scalps he'd seen with his Shoshoni family. Jimmy didn't understand why men — *tybo* or Indian — would do such things.

A distant scream interrupted his thoughts. He strained to hear above the thudding gallop of his horse. Dust blew across the trail carrying with it another high-pitched scream. Jimmy was puzzled until he looked north.

Less than a mile away, a stagecoach raced out of a canyon pulled by a team of panicked horses.

It veered off the trail, bouncing wildly through the sagebrush. To his horror, he realized the driver's box was empty. With no one to stop the coach, it could crash and there would be terrible injuries.

Jimmy knew he was the only one who could help, but to intercept the team he would have to detour from his route. An unwritten code of the Pony Express was to take care of mail first, horse second, self third. A rider must never slow down for anything or anyone else.

But Jimmy couldn't ignore people in trouble. Their screams of distress worried him.

His horse was fast. In a few minutes he was racing alongside the stage. An elderly man's face appeared at the open window, and that of a small boy. The thundering of hooves was deafening.

"Help us, sonny!" the man cried above the noise.

Jimmy wanted to leap into the driver's box, but it towered above his head. Instead he slipped his left foot out of the stirrup, then his right. Now he bounced in his saddle as he drew along the rear horse. Tensing his legs and arms, he jumped, landing awkwardly on the animal's rising back. He clutched the harness without looking at his own pony, which he hoped would stay nearby. It was important the *mochila* didn't get lost.

One set of reins flapped over the horse's ears in such a way that Jimmy could reach them by inching forward. He wrapped them around his fist and, while squeezing his legs against the horse so he wouldn't fall, he pulled back hard.

"Whoa, boys!" he yelled. "Whoa!"

They continued to run. Again Jimmy pulled. Finally the lead horse responded, but it began turning left. The harder Jimmy pulled, the sharper they turned. At this speed, the coach would flip over. If only he had his knife to slit the harness.

Suddenly Jimmy noticed a small figure to his right. It was a boy no more than ten years old. Somehow he had managed to crawl out the window and up to the roof of the swaying coach. He perched in the driver's box, trying to find the other set of reins. The brake lever was too low for him to reach.

"Careful!" Jimmy yelled, just as the boy managed to grab the thick leather straps. Pulling back as hard as his thin arms could and with Jimmy still pulling, the horses began to slow. In a moment they came to a stop in a spray of sand.

The door to the coach flew open and out tumbled another small boy, then his grandfather and two women, one holding a squalling infant. Jimmy was surprised there were so many children, but something surprised him more.

A girl his age, in a high-collared dress and white gloves, stepped out, opening a parasol as her foot touched the dirt.

Lillian Zimmerman. What on earth was the captain's daughter doing here? He was too astonished to speak.

"Oh, Jimmy," she cried, hurrying to his side. "I'm so glad to see you. Those wretched men — they bragged about being in Rex Dooley's gang — they shot our poor driver and they robbed every one of us of our valuables. Aunt Julia and I are on our way to Fort Churchill to see Father. . . . Oh, to think we were almost killed." Lillian burst into tears.

Jimmy felt uneasy, wanting to comfort her but not sure how. For several minutes they stood in the shade of the rear wheel, which was as tall as Jimmy. He noticed large parcels of mail strapped beneath the carriage, probably magazines and other letters too heavy for the *mochilas*. They were safe from robbers, but by the time the stage reached California everything would be soaked from river crossings.

Lillian brushed at the thick layers of dust on her dress and arranged her windblown hair. Jimmy thought she was pretty. He liked the way she smiled at him, even the way their arms bumped against each other. The nearness of her made him feel soft inside, and somehow lessened his desire for Nahanee. He didn't understand why this was.

He took Lillian's hand and as he helped her step up into the coach, he found himself flushed with pleasure. "We better get a move on," he said. "Mail's late and if we don't hurry, we'll be camping under the same stars as Rex Dooley."

10

WILD MUSTANGS

Jimmy and the grandfather drove the stage into Roberts Creek Station, arriving at sundown, the *mochila* safe on the seat beside them. A relief rider was waiting so Jimmy tossed the satchel to him. Mail was three hours behind schedule.

During the night a stable boy wiped off the coach so it was no longer brown with dust. At dawn it looked handsome with its bright red sides and gold lettering: WELLS, FARGO & CO. OVERLAND STAGE. Fresh horses flicked their tails and sniffed the cool morning air. Three new passengers joined the others.

Jimmy watched as they crowded aboard. He knew that those in the front and rear seats would be most comfortable because they could lean against the walls of the coach. Those on the narrow center bench had to hold onto leather loops suspended from the ceiling. Sitting knee-to-knee, their feet were crammed between canvas sacks and other cargo.

When the dust became unbearable for those facing forward, they could roll down the leather curtains or tie a kerchief over their mouths. Always there were arms touching arms and soon there would be the unpleasant odor of sweat and rancid breath. Drowsy heads would bump into shoulders.

Jimmy had heard of passengers going mad from lack of sleep or from other irritations. Dust. Heat. Motion sickness. Sometimes babies wouldn't stop crying and sometimes a person just talked too much.

Yes, that would do it, thought Jimmy. *Too much talk.* Suddenly he was filled with happiness. The endless blue sky reminded him of how free he was riding alone on a horse. Miles of open desert. Buttes purple in the distance. The wonderful sharp smell of sagebrush after a storm.

Cheerfully he saluted the stage's new driver as the man snapped the reins. The clopping of hooves and loud jangling of harnesses drowned out the cries of farewell. When Lillian leaned out the window and waved to Jimmy, he felt he was the luckiest boy alive.

After the noon meal Jimmy stepped out into the heat. Sand flies swarmed by the doorway, small and bothersome as ants. The blacksmith was shoeing a biting, squealing mustang, helped by three strong men. It would take them half a day to wrestle the animal down and nail the iron **U** onto each hoof.

Milo had explained that in the 1500s Spanish explorers rode these horses, calling them *mestengo*, meaning "wild." Mustangs were stocky with deep withers and broad flanks. They were especially valuable to the Pony Express because it had been learned that a grain diet gave them enough energy to outrun Indian ponies.

Just before supper, a rider sprinted into the yard and leaped off his horse yelling, "Trail's clear!" Three men restrained Jimmy's mount while another slipped the *mochila* over the saddle.

When he put his left foot in the stirrup, the horse reared and turned, swinging Jimmy out and to the side like a rag doll. He managed to pull himself up and grab the reins. The horse bucked twice, then reared again.

"This one's wild!" Jimmy cried to the blur of spectators. "How many times he been ridden?"

As the mustang bolted toward the trail, galloping full speed, Jimmy heard the stationmaster yell, "You're the first, Jimmy!"

11

AN EMBARRASSING MOMENT

On a cool September morning Jimmy relayed out of Roberts Creek. Dark clouds met the horizon and there was a rumble of thunder. When the first raindrop hit his neck, he shivered. It felt like ice.

Soon the hard-packed trail was muddy. Every few miles Jimmy shifted position in his saddle, but still his muscles ached as they had after his first ride in April. He sneezed. His fringed leather jacket felt heavy with the rain that now soaked his shirt, and his wet Levi's slipped against the *mochila*.

By the time Jimmy pulled in at Ruby Valley Station, he was chilled. How he wished he could soak in *Tosa-ibi*, the hot bubbling Soda Springs used by his Shoshoni family. This gave him an idea.

It would be several hours before he needed to

relieve the westbound rider, so there was time to rest. He hung his wet clothes on the rafters to dry. Still shivering, he set a tub in a corner near the north fireplace, which was warm with crackling piñon and a steamy black cauldron. Jimmy was thankful Milo and Mr. Tagg kept it filled with water and that they kept the woodpile high. It was not easy hauling logs from the hills above Ruby Lake.

The tub was actually a copper hip bath delivered by wagon from a society club in Salt Lake City. It looked like a coffee mug with its front scooped low. Jimmy could sit in it, water up to his hips, his legs draped over the sides. With his hat on his head to keep in body heat, he might be able to get rid of his chill.

Jimmy soaked luxuriously, eyes closed. The steam relaxed his aches and made him feel sleepy. His ears were so plugged up he did not hear the rumbling approach of a stagecoach. He did, however, feel a gust of cold air on his legs. When he looked up he saw Pen. He also saw Lillian Zimmerman hanging her shawl on a peg. She was chattering gaily about her visit to Fort Churchill. They had not noticed Jimmy in the corner.

Soon enough, though, Lillian turned. When she saw Jimmy's bare legs dangling over the tub, her hand flew to her cheek. "Oh, pardon me!" she cried.

Jimmy closed his eyes in despair. What was he supposed to do? He was exhausted. He had a runny nose and a terrible headache, which was why he couldn't think clearly. Yes, he was taking a bath, yes, Lillian Zimmerman was there. But the only logic he could make of that was to remember his father's stern advice:

Always stand when a lady enters the room.

With a splash, Jimmy lifted himself out of the tub, steam rising from his warm wet skin. After a few seconds of dripping on the dirt floor he realized his error and whisked his hat from his head down to his lap. Lillian's mouth dropped open. Pen immediately hid her eyes with his hand, spun her toward the door, and escorted her outside.

Miserable with embarrassment, Jimmy sank back into the tub. A few minutes later the stage pulled out and Pen returned, cold air sweeping into the room before he was able to close the door. "I'm terrible sorry, Jim," he said. "I had no idea you'd be taking a bath. Ain't she pretty though?"

Jimmy was groggy, but he managed a smile. Yes, she sure enough was.

"You gonna court Lillian when you get back to Salt Lake, Jimmy? She told me she likes you."

"I'm thinking on it. But I'm also thinking to go north come spring. Maybe."

Pen lifted the heavy pot from the coals and poured steaming water into Jimmy's tub. "To see your Indian family? What's that girl's name again?"

"Nahanee," said Jimmy. "We were good friends and I want to see her."

"But Jim, why would you think about courtin' an Indian when there're lots of girls in Salt Lake just dying for you to notice 'em? They smell good and have nice manners and being with them won't cause no controversy, if you know what I mean."

Jimmy sneezed. He lowered his shoulders into the hot water and closed his eyes. "It's hard to explain," he said with weariness. But somewhere inside Jimmy doubts were growing.

Maybe he should leave his past alone.

12

MR. LANTERN

By and by Jimmy's cold got better. Unless a rider was flat on his back or dead, he must get on his horse and go. Even though Jimmy didn't feel well, he continued his routes.

Late one chilly afternoon when he was rubbing down his horse, a Conestoga drawn by six mules stopped near the cabin. Several children peered out from the canvas cover.

"Welcome, strangers," called Mr. Tagg from the doorway. "Supper's almost ready. What we got is yours."

An assortment of young cousins jumped out of the wagon. A pretty woman with long red hair stepped down from the seat. She held an infant wrapped in a patchwork blanket. Another woman was round and heavy with child.

"Obliged," the driver said, reaching to shake hands all around. His large black hat made his eyes look dark. "Hank Lantern's the name and these here are my kin. We'll be movin' out by sunrise tomorrow if you all don't mind us bedding down in your front yard for the night."

Milo passed a cup of coffee to him. "Well, sir, that's all right by us, but it's somewhat peculiar you folks are headin' west this late in the season. The Donner Party — wasn't that in '46, Mr. Tagg? Yes? — well, they took the Hastings Cutoff this time of year hoping to make it over the Sierra before the big snows. Tragic. I never realized decent human beings could turn into cannibals."

"I heard about them. But we'll be all right, long as we don't dawdle. My brother and nine other families are waiting for us at Rag Town. We'll be all right."

While the men talked, Pen and Jimmy led the mules to the corral. They could see the women cleaning out the wagon as their children played hide-and-seek in the brush.

"Jim, don't it look like that one lady is gonna have a baby?"

"Looks that way to me."

"Well, where's she gonna have it?"

Jimmy shrugged. "Somewhere between here and Californy, I suspect."

They unharnessed the mules, spread fresh hay

for them, then saw to their water. Pen buttoned his coat against the chill and rubbed his hands together. "You ever wonder, Jim, why folks travel so far with every possession they have, just to look for a better place, not knowing for sure if there is one?"

"Seems all kinds of folks do it," said Jimmy. "My pa did, moved us from New York to Salt Lake City. And when I was with Washakie, the tribe moved all the time, but it was with the seasons and to follow game. Sometimes they came here to Ruby Valley, but it wasn't because one place was better than another."

Pen looked at his friend with fascination, wanting to hear more. "But didn't you get homesick for your own family?" he asked.

"At first, yes. But then it was as if I'd always lived with the Shoshoni. They became my family and I didn't want to leave."

Pen knew Jimmy had returned to Salt Lake so people could see he hadn't been kidnapped or held against his will. "Jim," he said, "if you liked it so much, living with the Indians, why didn't you go back 'soon as your folks saw you were all right?"

"I'm not sure, Pen." Jimmy closed the corral gate, then turned toward the cabin. Smoke curling up in the cool air smelled like supper. "I didn't want to disappoint my mother and father again, and somehow that was enough to keep me home."

"So what's holding you back now?"

"I keep asking myself that. One thing, I made a

commitment to Mr. Majors, and another thing . . ." Jimmy sighed. His breath made frost. "Oh, never mind. We better go warn Mr. Lantern not to take Shadow Canyon. There're Paiutes everywhere."

13

A MOTHER'S GIFT

Just before noon a galloping horseman appeared in the west, heading for Ruby Valley so fast its dust was far behind the pony's flared tail. Tight in the saddle was fourteen-year-old Billy Cody, one of the youngest Pony Express riders. Within minutes he drew to a stop in a spray of dirt.

"There're some crazy travelers out there," he cried, leaping to the ground. "I circled their wagon to warn the driver, but he kept going."

Billy was small and thin and looked too young to be riding alone in the vast, empty desert. He searched the faces around him for reassurance. "Can't we do something? Those folks're headed straight for Shadow Canyon and there's a war party waiting for 'em, Indians everywhere! I told the man but he just kept on going."

Milo yanked off his hat in frustration and slapped it against his leg. "That miserable fool," he cried. "How can a man be so pigheaded plumb stupid? We told Mr. Lantern not to take the shortcut, we told him to go south of Shadow Canyon, not through it. We warned him, but he didn't listen."

Jimmy looked worried as he dipped a cup into the water barrel and offered it to the small boy. They had become friends during the brief times they shared layovers. "How'd you get through, Billy?" he asked him.

"Same as always. Laid low and beat it. Lost my hat, though. I felt it go *pow* off my head like I'd been shot. *Pow*, just like that. And it was my white straw one, too, cost me three dollars. Say, when're you up, Spoon?"

"Any minute. I think Pen Hailey's got the leg from Deep Creek. Oh, I wish he'd get here now; someone's gotta make Mr. Lantern turn around."

Nearly an hour later, Milo yelled from the corral. "Jim! You're up!"

There were shouts and a flurry of dust as a fresh horse, its westbound mail, and Jimmy raced away.

The faster his horse sped on, the smoother the ride. Jimmy felt that if he were a bird, this is what it would be like to fly. The wind in his face was cold and his hair blew loose behind his collar. He had a shoelace tied under his chin to keep his hat on. Crouched low like this he could feel the sting-ing ends of the mane.

He knew he could catch Mr. Lantern, he *had* to catch him. If Jimmy could stop a runaway stage, surely he could stop six slow mules.

But after several miles, he did not see any trace of the prairie schooner. The trail was beginning to narrow in its steep approach to Shadow Canyon. He slowed his horse hoping to see or hear some-thing, anything that would be a clue to what lay ahead. If Mr. Lantern had made it through, then Jimmy would need to hurry for his own safety.

The trail wound through a sandy gulch into the canyon. Three feet on either side of him rose sheer rock walls that at every hour except high noon cast deep shadows. It was always cool in Shadow Canyon.

There were fresh wheel tracks, fresh, Jimmy knew, because the wind had not yet smoothed their edges.

He looked up and around, fearful someone might be watching him, waiting. When he saw the man's hat in the dirt, pinned by a two-foot-long arrow, Jimmy's heart sank.

It was a black hat.

Filled with dread, he stopped. Ahead, the trail widened into a protected campsite. He knew Paiutes hunted here and took refuge from the heat. Desert bighorn sheep lived among the rocks as did mountain lions and bobcats. Golden eagles nested in the cliffs. A thin waterfall splashed down into a clear, deep pool. To Jimmy it was the most beautiful oasis in the desert, but at this moment it was the most horrible place ever.

Several yards around the bend, he saw the wagon. The mules were gone. When he saw the bodies he quickly turned away and squeezed his eyes shut. He knew from the blood and from the way they were sprawled, that all were dead. His horse snorted and began stepping with nervousness. It had caught their scent on the breeze.

"Fool!" Jimmy screamed to the cliffs. "Stupid man!" Enraged and filled with sorrow he buried his face in the long, tangled mane and wept. Jimmy was heartsick. Why hadn't Mr. Lantern listened to him? And why did Indians have to murder these innocent people?

Jimmy needed to think and to pray before he'd be able to gather the courage to bury the poor family. An unspoken code among travelers was that death would be dignified by burial, whether by friend or stranger, before vultures and coyotes took over.

Still unable to look toward the wagon, he kneeled in the sand. The mustang seemed to understand it was not to run off. It nuzzled Jimmy's neck as if to comfort him.

Above the sound of the waterfall Jimmy heard a faint cry, as if a kitten were mewing. He lifted his head to listen. It mewed again. Cautiously he stood up, tied the reins to a branch, then began moving toward a cluster of rocks near the pond. He wished he had one of Jack Slade's ivory-handled revolvers.

When Jimmy peered inside a low, small cave he couldn't believe his eyes. There was a baby, a live human baby wrapped in a patchwork quilt. It had red hair. Its cheeks were puffy from crying and its voice was so hoarse it squeaked like a kitten.

Jimmy reached in and tenderly scooped the bundle into his arms. Instantly he forgot about the horror behind him. His anger at Mr. Lantern was replaced by admiration for the baby's mother who had managed to hide her child safely. Apparently the Indians had not heard it crying.

"Easy, fella, easy." Jimmy used the same gentle words he used with horses, and it seemed to work. The infant gazed up at him. Its cries softened to hiccups.

Jimmy knew he needed to get the baby to safety. There was no time to bury the family.

He dipped his hand in the stream and let water drip off his fingers into the tiny mouth. Its tongue was swollen from thirst, but it was able to drink. Old Mother had shown this trick to Jimmy when they once found an orphaned papoose. This memory deepened the affection he felt for her.

Even though the air was cold, Jimmy took off his shirt. He tied it into a sling so the baby could ride securely against his chest. The horse was perfectly still while Jimmy pulled himself into the saddle, as if it, too, wanted to protect its new passenger.

14

ROBERTS CREEK STATION

The men who helped Jimmy change horses at Sulphur Creek were astonished to see a child wrapped in his shirt. But they cheered and threw their hats in the air when Jimmy managed, within two minutes, to return to the trail for his ride to Roberts Creek Station. Mrs. Roberts was one of the few women in the territory who had a baby and if anyone would know what to do with an extra one, she would.

The smooth rocking gait of the horse was like a cradle. The infant did not wake up until it found itself in the arms of Mrs. Roberts, with a dozen strange faces smiling down at it. Immediately its mouth wrinkled and it began to cry.

Jimmy was so exhausted he sat down on an upturned crate where he could see out the window to the corral. It was a cool autumn day. Soldiers from Major Hendrick's battalion were readying their horses for Shadow Canyon, for burial duty. They would bring back any personal items that might help them locate the baby's relatives.

"It's a boy, Jim," called Mrs. Roberts, "about five months old, same as my Lucy. Since you found 'im, you get the honor of naming 'im."

The scene reminded Jimmy of Old Mother and he suddenly found himself thinking in the Shoshoni language.

"*Ingabumbee,*" he said out loud. His beloved Old Mother would have named him Ingabumbee, Red Hair. He felt tears sting his eyes.

Mrs. Roberts returned to her work at the stove with Ingabumbee riding in her arm as if he had been hers all along. When he began to howl with hunger — a different cry than when he was startled by strangers — Mrs. Roberts tucked him under her bib apron and opened her blouse so he could nurse, his head supported in the crook of her left arm.

With her right hand she carried an iron skillet sizzling with potatoes and ham. She set it on the table, pulled a long-handled spoon from her apron pocket, then began serving the travelers. All this she did with quiet dignity.

Jimmy had seen Shoshoni women do the same. They cared for one another's children without question, nursing them while a mother slept or adopting them completely. There were no orphans among Indian people.

After supper Jimmy moved the crate he'd been sitting on and turned it over next to Lucy's box, which was near the fireplace. With the patchwork quilt he made a soft cozy cradle. He was amused to see Ingabumbee propped against Mrs. Roberts's shoulder. The baby's fuzzy red hair stood straight up, and he was looking wide-eyed around him as she stacked dishes with her free hand. She brought to the table a bowl of sweet, yellow apples.

Jimmy took the boy. He wanted to help Mrs. Roberts as he had helped Hanabi with baby Oddo and his own mother with little Thomas. They were all the same, babies were. They needed to eat, sleep, and be rocked. He knew the men in the room were staring at him, but he didn't care.

Washakie hadn't laughed when Jimmy swept out Hanabi's tipi or when he did chores that only women were supposed to do. He was proud he remembered the chief's words: "If you can do good to someone, do it. It does not hurt for us to help one another."

15

TWO SOUTHERN GENTLEMEN

One of the men in the crowded room sat by the hearth, turned toward the firelight. He was writing in a small brown notebook with a stub pencil. He kept glancing at Jimmy and Ingabumbee as if he were making notes about them. His reddish-brown hair was wild, and his bushy mustache was speckled with bits of potato left over from supper. A leather satchel at his side had the name SAM CLEMENS engraved on the handle.

The odd thing about Mr. Clemens and the man next to him was that they were wearing only their short-sleeved underwear and their boots.

Mr. Clemens acknowledged Jimmy with a nod, then cleared his throat as if preparing to deliver a speech. "You seem curious about our attire," he began. "When we left St. Joe, my brother and I could not keep the dust out of our coach. Happily there were no ladies aboard so the intelligent solution, of course, was for us to disrobe and continue the journey in our Skivvies. We are southern gentlemen on our way to Carson City. In clean clothes, the governor will not mistake us for ruffians."

The blacksmith standing at the other end of the hearth leaned forward to get a better look at them. He was a large man with thick arms. He was picking ham out of his teeth with his fingernail. "You mean you two dandies rode clear to Roberts Crik in your underwear just so's you wouldn't get dirty? Why, Rex Dooley and his gang gets a bounty for scoundrels like you!" He roared with laughter and slammed his fist onto the mantel, which prompted the soldiers and other travelers — all men — to erupt in jeers.

The noise in the room was deafening. Jimmy tensed, expecting a fight to break out. Quickly he tucked Ingabumbee into his cradle. But the Clemens brothers had taken no offense; in fact they roared and stomped their boots right along with the others. Dust from the floor rose in the smoky room.

Soon it was evident to Jimmy that the two southern gentlemen dressed in Skivvies were not gentlemen at all. They were loud and they cussed. They spit on the floor. Jimmy's eyes widened when the two began telling jokes about polygamous men in Salt Lake City. They criticized the Mormon president.

"He never paid any attention to me," Sam complained. "Brigham Young was like an old cat who looked around to see which kitten was meddling with his tail. He seemed bored with us, utterly bored."

Apparently Brigham Young had not been impressed with the brothers. Maybe he had heard them make fun of his wives, or maybe they bragged too much about their jobs in Carson City. Or maybe they had forgotten to put on their shirts and trousers.

Jimmy stepped outside. There was still a blush over the western mountains where the sun had set an hour before. The air was frosty and he could see his breath. He walked to the corral. He loved it out here, away from the noise, with the comforting smell of horses and hay.

He leaned over the rough log railing and clicked his tongue. Two mares lifted their heads, considered him for a moment, then trotted over. From his shirt pocket he took out an apple. He pressed his thumb by the stem, down, until the apple split neatly in half.

"Here, girls," he said. "Easy."

While they ate, Jimmy watched the sky. Stars began appearing in the growing darkness. *Shadow Canyon must be cold and empty now*, he thought. He felt sad about Mr. Lantern and his poor family, sad that Ingabumbee lost his mother.

Lamplight glowed from the cabin's windows. When someone opened the door, laughter swelled out into the night, then faded again as the door closed. Safe inside, the baby slept. Jimmy's spirits lifted when he realized he would be able to see Ingabumbee every time he rode into Roberts Creek. Maybe someday he would take the boy north to visit his Shoshoni family.

Old Mother would love to meet a little red-haired child, and so would Nahanee, beautiful Nahanee.

Jimmy kicked a fence post in frustration. If only he could stop thinking about them.

16

CHRISTMAS EVE, 1860

A cold wind blew across Ruby Valley. Weeds poking above the snow marked the sides of the trail. Frost stung Jimmy's cheeks, making him wish he could grow whiskers to keep his face warm. He wished he had the muskrat hat and the tall furry moccasins that his dear Old Mother had sewn for him.

Around his neck he wore a gray wool scarf that itched and, under his clothes, wool long johns, also itchy. Buckskin gloves kept his hands from freezing, but by the time he would unsaddle his horse, his fingers would be too numb to hold a soup spoon.

How grateful Jimmy was to sit in front of the fire. Snow blew in through narrow cracks in the walls, melting on the floor into small muddy pools. Often others were there, too, warming themselves between rides, sometimes new boys who'd just been hired, sometimes travelers. It was easy to make friends around a fire, as it had been around the fire in Washakie's tipi. To Jimmy, there was nothing like a cozy, warm lodge in a blizzard.

One snowy evening Pen and Jimmy wrapped bread dough around twigs and held them over the coals to bake. When done, they passed one to Billy Cody who dozed in a bunk, one to Mr. Tagg, and one to another boy named Gus. While they ate the delicious hot stickbread, Milo brought his Bible to the hearth. It was identical to Jimmy's, small as a hand, and bound in soft dark suede.

"Don't s'pose you realize this," he said, "but it's a special night. It's Christmas Eve. I'd like to read you fellas something." He and Mr. Tagg still had not taken a bath or washed their hair, but Jimmy didn't mind. They could cook and they spoiled the boys as if they were grandsons.

Milo sat on a three-legged stool, elbows on his knees. His voice was soothing as he read from the book of Luke, the story of the Christ Child, the Messiah. Jimmy felt safe and warm. He wanted to sleep.

Too soon Mr. Tagg was shaking his shoulder. "You're up, Jim. Drink this cocoa, hurry. It's stopped snowing, but the wind's pickin' up."

Jimmy didn't want to leave the warm cabin. For the first time since he took the job, he did not care if mail took ten days or ten years, and he no longer cared about being a hero. It wasn't as much fun as he'd thought it would be.

The more Jimmy thought about going out into the cold, the more unhappy he became. No wonder other boys had quit. Many hadn't been paid in months. There was never enough time to sleep or warm up or just lounge around the fire with friends. Mr. Majors had given them Bibles, but he'd forgotten they would need time to read them.

Outlaws and Indians were a hazard and so were some travelers. There were several instances where nervous emigrants fired shots at speeding ponies, mistaking them for Paiutes' ponies. Another worry was riding at night. Jimmy didn't want to admit this to anyone, but being alone in the pitch-dark scared him.

When Milo saw Jimmy's sour face, he set the Bible down and grabbed his coat off a bunk. He opened the door for Jimmy, and together they stepped out into the cold where their breath turned to frost. The black sky was alive with stars. They could hear the drumming hooves of the westbound rider, approaching fast. As a grandfather might do, Milo checked Jimmy's scarf to make sure it covered his throat and neck, then gave his shoulders a quick hug.

In the next rushing moments while Mr. Tagg caught the *mochila* and Jimmy mounted, Milo called, "We need you, son. We're all countin' on you."

In a bolt, Jimmy was off. The rush of cold air woke him completely and made him crouch close to the horse for warmth. Wind drove a chill into his arms and legs as if he'd been wearing no clothes at all, but for some reason he felt excited. The night was beautiful. Snow made the desert look like a white quilt. In the pale darkness, the trail resembled a long narrow seam running between the quilt's downy folds.

Jimmy suddenly felt privileged to be out in the cold, riding a horse under stars so brilliant he wanted to shout to their Creator with joy. The things he'd been upset about earlier now seemed small. Folks were counting on him. It was Christmas Eve and he had a job to do.

17

WAR IN THE EAST

Winter was bitterly cold.

Three Gosiute hunters were found near Ruby Lake, frozen to death and starved, apparently on their way to ask for food. During the same blizzard, Pen Hailey's horse fell in a hole and broke its neck. In waist-deep snow Pen walked the *mochila* three miles to the next station. He arrived nearly frozen himself.

Several boys quit because they decided they weren't being paid enough. Some quit because they'd hurt themselves and others quit to help finish the transcontinental telegraph. Poles were being planted west of the Missouri River at such a rate that soon wires would reach coast to coast.

In winter, loneliness was sharper. Wind howled

across the desert, blowing snow over the trail and into tall drifts against the cabin. Visitors were few. Friends were separated for days at a time while they rode in opposite directions. Sometimes a relief boy would be in bed with fever. This meant the tired rider must carry the *mochila* another fifty or even another hundred miles, stopping only to change horses and drink a bit of water.

Riders leaving St. Joseph often shouted news items to every station they passed. Like paperboys on street corners, they cried the headlines all the way to Sacramento:

"President Buchanan's Farewell Address to Congress!"

"Texas Leaves the Union!"

"Kansas Gets Its Statehood!"

"Congress Makes a Territory for Colorado!"

" . . . Nevada!"

" . . . Dakota!"

Then spring came and with it the event that sparked the quickest run ever — seven days, seventeen hours. Every boy and horse was pushed to go as fast as possible, so fast that two mustangs were galloped to death. Riders raced in pairs for safety, shouting together the word from Washington City: "Lincoln's Inaugural Address!"

Less than two weeks after Abraham Lincoln was sworn in as the sixteenth president of the United States, his speech was printed in San Francisco newspapers. No longer would Americans joke that news had already been forgotten in the east by the time folks in the west heard it.

One month later, when Jimmy learned that Confederates had fired on Fort Sumter in South Carolina, he had a bad feeling. He knew it meant civil war.

No one in the dusty way stations could foresee that this fighting between Northern and Southern states would last four long, terrible years. No one realized that hundreds of thousands would die.

After Jimmy shouted this story on a night run all the way to Roberts Creek Station, he returned to Ruby Valley the next morning in time for breakfast. Smoke wisping from the chimney brought the good smell of bacon frying and griddle cakes. He was famished. He couldn't wait to eat and to talk politics with Milo or whoever else was at the table.

But when he entered the cabin his heart sank. His friends Will and Nick Cone were rolling up their gear. Their boots were clean and they wore bright red bandanas with shirts that Mr. Tagg had washed and mended for them. Their young faces were eager.

"Jim!" they cried, happy to see him.

But Jimmy didn't smile. He looked at Milo, then back at his friends. "What're you fellas doing? Why are you packing?"

"We're going to war!" Nick announced. "Jimmy, we're going to be soldiers, real soldiers. The Confederates need us."

Jimmy's shoulders dropped. "Why do you want to go to war? Why?" He squeezed his hands into fists, trying to think of words to discourage them. The memory of Washakie's war with the Crow was

72

still a horrible scar inside him. Men died in wars. They were mutilated or crippled or blinded. Mothers would lose sons and brothers; they would lose husbands. How could Jimmy explain?

"We'll be heroes, Jim."

"Heroes?" Jimmy said, almost with a laugh. "You already are heroes, why do you wanna be heroes twice? You're riders for the Pony Express, like me and Pen, remember? We joined up together; we promised we'd stay together." He gestured to Milo as if to say, *Can't you stop them?*, but Milo and Mr. Tagg remained silent. Their eyes were sad.

A clatter from the approaching stage interrupted Jimmy. Before he could protest, the two excited brothers hurried out into the brisk April morning. While a fresh team was harnessed to the coach, Nick and Will tossed their bundles into the rear boot. They tried to console Jimmy.

"We'll be back to Salt Lake before you know it," said Will. "We got kin in Georgia so we'll be all right. Don't frown so, Jim, it'll go fast."

Slowly Jimmy took Will's hand, then Nick's. He wanted to embrace them both, but hesitated when he noticed passengers watching. Among them were three young riders, spiffed up and smiling like boys headed for war. Sam Melvin, Johnny Fry, and another boy he didn't know had quit the Pony and were going east to join the army. Jimmy wondered if they were breaking their contracts.

The dusty red coach pulled out. Arms waving out each side made it look like a strange creature scurrying away. Clouds of powdery white alkali rose from the trail as it sped on. Jimmy's heart was heavy. He would miss his friends and he would worry about them.

He wandered beyond the corral out into the sandy brush. After many minutes Mr. Tagg came looking for him, wiping his calloused hands on his apron.

"Come on in now, son," he said gently. "I know how you feel . . . I wish they weren't going myself. Milo and I each lost a brother at the Alamo in '36. That battle was terrible for so many families. Alls we can do, Jim, is ask the Lord to watch over Nick and Willie. That's all we can do."

18

AN OLD FRIEND

As the snow began to melt, wagons with families resumed their westward journeys. When Jimmy's bunk was needed for elderly or ill travelers, he and Pen slept outdoors. Near the corral they made a wide bed of hay three feet high. There they slept burrowed down out of the wind, wrapped in wool blankets, stars overhead.

Early one morning, when the eastern sky began to pale, Jimmy woke suddenly. For a moment he lay there, frightened, his heart racing. He listened.

Pen slept next to him, a light snore ruffling from his open mouth. Slowly Jimmy started to sit up, but as he did, something held his right arm down. When he saw the arrow, he fell back with a groan.

"Pen," he whispered, kicking his friend's foot. "Wake up, *get up*. I've been shot."

Another kick and Pen bolted upright. His curly blond hair was full of straw. Sleepily he bent over Jimmy, who was still moaning. His eyes strained in the darkness to see the wound, but when Pen touched the arrow, he realized it had only pierced the wide sleeve of Jimmy's shirt. It had plunged into the straw, missing his arm by inches.

Seeing an opportunity to play a trick, Pen shook his head, pretending to be sad. "They got you good this time, Jimmy. Mr. Tagg's gonna have to amputate. I'll fetch his hacksaw . . ."

"Wait, don't leave me!" cried Jimmy, but when he heard Pen snort with laughter, he took a better look at his arm. Secretly he hoped there would be blood or some kind of wound, even a scratch would do. But the only damage was that his sleeve tore when he yanked out the arrow. He gave Pen a playful shove.

"Quit it, we coulda both been scal — "

"You shoulda seen your face, Jim, you shoulda seen it. Like this," and Pen raised his eyebrows in mock horror, again collapsing in laughter.

Jimmy was embarrassed. He also was a little disappointed their haystack wasn't riddled with arrows, to prove they'd almost been killed. It would have made a splendid story to scare Lillian Zimmerman.

The gray dawn was cold. Jimmy settled deeper into the straw where it was warm. He studied the arrow. The shaft was smooth cherry wood, about eighteen inches long, and the tip was metal, not stone. This meant the tribe had been trading with white men for some time.

The feathers on the end were bluish, from the wings of a mountain bluebird. Jimmy felt a tingle of recognition. These past months on the desert, he had not seen one mountain bluebird. But he had seen them years ago, further north, in the land of the Shoshoni and Bannocks.

Jimmy looked closer. In the growing light he could see markings below the feathers. Slowly he rolled the arrow between his fingers. There were tiny scratches in the shape of *nampa*, a moccasin.

A wild joy rose inside Jimmy. He jumped to his feet and turned toward the cottonwoods that surrounded the oasis. In the shadows he thought he saw a horseman, watching. Jimmy raised the arrow over his head. In response, a cry came from the trees, the cry of a bluebird taking flight.

Jimmy's eyes filled. Nampa had found him. He was in the woods and he wanted Jimmy to follow.

19

A MESSAGE FOR JIMMY

Jimmy quickly shook out his boots in case of scorpions, then slipped them onto his bare feet.

"I'll be back," he called to Pen as he began running along the narrow trail. A black-tailed jackrabbit bounded out of the brush as he reached the oasis. Jimmy could smell Nampa before he saw him, a rich musky smell that reminded him of deerskin shirts, bear grease, and the smoky fires inside tipis.

"Dawii," came the familiar voice as Nampa slid off his horse and stepped into the clearing. For a moment they studied each other, then they rushed forward with a handshake that became a crushing embrace, the embrace of old friends.

Nampa laughed. "Scared you good, didn't I, Dawii?"

"Naw. I knew it was you all along."

Jimmy was surprised how easily he answered in Shoshoni, as if only yesterday he had left the tribe. He was more surprised though, that the Nampa who now stood before him was a young man. He wore buckskin leggings, fringed on the sides, and moccasins with a double row of blue beads across the toe. His bare chest was broader and his arms more muscular.

A thick scar ran from Nampa's left elbow up to his neck. Jimmy knew this wound was recent because it was shiny pink, and he wondered if Nampa had been hurt in battle.

His braids hung to his waist, the ends wrapped in strips of red cloth. His pompadour was brushed up high from his forehead with grease. A lock of hair by each ear was adorned with beads and tin rings. Nampa was a handsome fellow.

While they looked at each other with silent admiration, Jimmy felt a thrill. Nearly five years ago they had parted as fourteen-year-old boys. *Now Nampa and I are men*, he thought.

With a gesture from Nampa they sat down. A breeze stirred the leaves of the cottonwoods, a whisper in the otherwise still air. In the east, the orange tip of the sun rose above the horizon with a burst of light. The day had begun. Finally Nampa spoke.

"Old Mother is ill," he said. "She has lost her

sight and her breath is weak. She grieves for her *tybo* son who has not returned."

Jimmy's mouth went dry. He looked at Nampa with eyes that asked, *How much longer will she live?*

Nampa's high cheekbones made his face appear strong; gone was the roundness of boyhood. After several long moments he answered, "One, maybe two moons."

Jimmy turned away. He was heartsick and at the same time furious with himself. *Why hadn't he gone back to his Shoshoni family sooner?* If he hadn't been so busy being a hero he might already be sitting with Old Mother in her tipi, helping to keep her fire warm. He could be carrying water for her in the little brass bucket she loved so much.

"Nampa, old friend, tell her I am coming. I will leave in three sleeps." Jimmy stood. He needed to tell Milo and Mr. Tagg, for his year contract was nearly up anyway. Three days would be long enough for them to find a rider to replace him. It would be enough time to rest his horse, to prepare for the long journey north.

Something else. The moment Jimmy saw Nampa, every doubt he'd ever had, vanished. He would return to the Shoshoni. More than anything in the world, he wanted to return.

20

THIEVES IN THE NIGHT

When Jimmy rode back from Roberts Creek the next evening, Milo hurried him inside and pressed a rifle into his arms.

"Paiutes, Jim. They're camped at Ruby Lake."

Jimmy was tired and hungry. He did not want there to be any fighting. "Maybe they're just hunting," he said, taking a seat at the table.

"Well, that would be all right by me, but these fellas are painted for war."

The sound of a horse squealing interrupted them, then there was the rumble of galloping hooves.

"The ponies!" Jimmy cried. He flung open the door and raced out into the darkness, cocking the rifle as he ran. He fired two warning shots, then tossed the gun to Milo. "Cover me!"

Jimmy ran. He could see the dim outline of the corral, the moving shapes of men and mustangs leaping over a broken rail. It would be impossible to stop them, he knew this, but he had to try. Without horses, the mail would be delayed. Without a horse, Jimmy wouldn't be able to follow Nampa in two days as he had planned.

When he stumbled, he thought at first he'd bumped his head on a post. The pain brought him to his knees. He reached up to touch where it hurt, above his right eye, but there was something there — a stick. Then the ground met his back and he found himself staring up into the blurred face of Milo. Jimmy opened his mouth to speak, but no words came.

"Stay put, Jimmy, stay right there, don't move." Then under his breath Milo said, "Lord in heaven, we need your help."

Jimmy was aware of being carried into the cabin, of voices leaning over him. Only when he heard a snap, followed by a searing pain, did he realize Milo was trying to pull an arrow out of his skull. Again Jimmy's hand moved up, to feel the wound, as if by doing so it would help the sting go away.

But Mr. Tagg tied his arms to the bed, then his legs. He whispered in Jimmy's ear, "I'm so sorry to do this to you, son, but we need you to stop kicking. Milo's got to get that arrowhead out before it poisons you."

As Jimmy drifted into unconsciousness he felt as if he were still running, trying to catch his horse. He wanted to call for Nampa. *"Tell Old Mother I'm coming,* '' he tried to yell. But he lacked the strength, and his voice was no louder than a whisper.

A distraught Pen Hailey was now at Jimmy's side, kneeling on the cold dirt floor. His hands were folded in prayer and as he looked heavenward, tears ran down his cheeks.

"Lord, don't let Jimmy die. Please."

Twenty minutes after midnight Billy Cody rode in from Deep Creek. When Mr. Tagg met him out by the empty corral, he gave him the bad news. Billy led his horse to water, then hurried into the stationhouse. He bent over his injured friend and, after getting a good look, turned wide-eyed to the others.

"Is he dead?" he asked.

"Not yet."

"He needs help. I'll fetch Doc Miller at Thorny Crik. Hang on, Spoon, hang on!" Billy drank a quick cup of water, then dashed out into the starry night.

His horse responded so swiftly that, by the time Mr. Tagg waved good-bye, they had become a small dark shape in the distance.

21

A MARRIAGE PROPOSAL

Jimmy didn't regain consciousness for six days. On the seventh morning his eyes opened. He tried to sit up, but his head throbbed as if a stone were bouncing inside his skull. A thick bandage prevented him from touching the wound.

When Milo saw Jimmy looking around, he jumped up from his stool. "Praise God," he cried. "The doc said you were a goner, but we refused to believe him. Jimmy, we've all been prayin' round the clock. Mr. Tagg," he yelled out the doorway, "Mr. Tagg, hurry. Jimmy's awake!"

By late afternoon Jimmy had managed to take a few steps by leaning against the bed rails. Though his left arm hung limp at his side and his left leg dragged, a smile was on his face. He didn't remember being shot, but he did remember Nampa's visit.

"Milo," he said slowly, "get my horse. I'm ready to leave."

It was evident to Milo that Jimmy wouldn't be able to walk on his own, let alone ride a horse several hundred miles north, but he did not want to discourage him. "Well, son, I guess you are ready," he said cheerfully. He offered Jimmy his elbow and helped him shuffle outside. Eight new horses were in the corral. The charred remains of one of the sheds was the only evidence that Ruby Valley Station had been attacked by Paiutes.

Jimmy stopped by the watering trough. Though the sun was low in the sky, its brightness hurt his eyes and made him so dizzy he began to weave. Milo caught him as he fell, then, in his strong arms, carried Jimmy back to his bunk.

"Well," Jimmy said as Milo gently tucked a pillow under his head. "Maybe I won't leave just yet. Maybe I'll have a bite of supper first."

"Now that's a right good idea, son. Mr. Tagg is making your favorite stew and we would all be mighty honored to have you at our table tonight."

Jimmy slept for seven more days and nights, waking only long enough to sip soup and be helped outside to relieve himself. Riders came and went, stagecoaches, too. Letters for Jimmy arrived in the *mochila*'s way pocket, the front right pouch that carried personal mail for each way station. Each stationmaster had a key to its little brass padlock.

When Lillian Zimmerman's perfumed envelope
arrived, everyone in the room hovered near
Jimmy, hoping he would read it aloud. It wasn't
often that a girl would write one of the boys. Her
letter — which had cost five dollars in postage —
had been written on one sheet of tissue paper, both
sides, in print so small Mr. Tagg had to put on his
spectacles to help. Lillian's words were crowded
into every possible space, sideways in margins,
then upside down between lines. Mr. Tagg turned
the letter here and there, squinting as if decoding
a map. Finally he cleared his throat. " *'Dear
Jimmy,' '* he began.

" *'We are all most horribly sorry about your mishap
with the Indians and hope you'll soon come home to
meet your new baby brother. His name is John. He is
as fat as a little potato and he looks just like Thomas.
Your mother is busy.*

" *'Your sisters Clara and Molly married Ezra Smith
on the twenty-first and twenty-eighth of March respec-
tively. I should think they are happy, even though Mr.
Smith already has two other wives under the same roof.
I personally plan not to share a husband's affections,
and I would like to know if this is all right with you,
Jimmy . . .'* " At this, Mr. Tagg stopped. His bushy
white eyebrows raised in surprise.

"Why, Jim," he said, "if you'll forgive my edi-
torial comment here, I do believe Miss Lillian is
proposing marriage." He looked at the faces
around him for confirmation.

Milo, who was on his stool nursing a mug of
coffee, nodded slowly. "Yes, sir, I do believe that

is what the young lady is trying to convey."

All eyes turned to Jimmy. He was sitting up in his bunk. Color had returned to his cheeks and the wound above his eye was a healthy pink. He didn't know what to make of Lillian's letter, except that he was pleased to hear his mother was well and that he had a new baby brother.

This made him think about his dear old Shoshone mother. How he missed her. She had been so kind and gentle to Jimmy. She had taught him so much. It wasn't fair that she was near death.

Now something else occurred to him. Jimmy had been so concerned about Old Mother's poor health that he'd forgotten to ask Nampa about Nahanee. He realized with a sudden race of his heart that she, too, would be five years older. She would be past the age when many Shoshoni girls married.

Nahanee. He must see her again. While his friends watched with concern, Jimmy eased himself off his bunk and braced himself against the table.

His throat was so tight, he swallowed hard to keep the lump down. "Can someone please help me get on my horse? I have to go north."

22

JIMMY'S SMALL VISITOR

Jimmy draped his arms over the corral gate and watched Mr. Tagg unsaddle the horses. It had been wonderful to ride again even though the bouncing at first made his head pound. But Milo had been firm: Jimmy was not ready to take on such a long journey alone; he would need to rest several more weeks.

Those stern words had filled Jimmy with despair. *Several more weeks.* By now Nampa would have returned to the Shoshoni camps and told Old Mother that Dawii was coming in three sleeps. She would be waiting for him, listening to every footstep that passed her tipi. Jimmy couldn't stand the thought of her dying. And worst of all, that she might die thinking he had broken a promise.

Also, there was Nahanee. Jimmy wasn't sure what he expected or wanted from the beautiful girl who had been his friend. All he knew was he wanted to be with her.

Someone was whistling "Yankee Doodle." Jimmy turned to see Pen boost himself onto the gate. His face was beaming. "Jim, you can leave in three days instead of three weeks and I know how!"

Jimmy looked up at his friend. There were bits of straw and leaves in the curly hair that Pen had trouble remembering to comb. His brown eyes were merry.

"What're you talking about?" Jimmy asked him, cautious.

"Milo just told me two more riders are being assigned to Ruby Valley on account of Billy Cody's hurt foot and one just for good measure. Think, Jim."

Jimmy gazed at a cloud for a moment, trying to understand. Finally he broke into a smile.

"Three days means a full moon. Are you coming with me, Pen?"

"If you'll let me."

"Will I!"

On a cool morning in May, a few days before Jimmy's nineteenth birthday, he and Pen gathered their gear. They planned to leave after the noon meal. For the first time in a year, Jimmy took out his eagle feather and tied it to the brim of his hat. Shoshoni honored the eagle as a symbol of strength and protection, and now that he was keeping his promise, Jimmy felt worthy to wear it.

From outside came Mr. Tagg's voice, announcing a visitor. Soon a wagon drawn by two mules pulled up in front of the cabin. When Mrs. Roberts swept down from the driver's seat, she pushed her sunbonnet back so it hung behind her. A large basket covered with gingham was on her left arm.

"Jimmy Spoon," she called. "You're not leaving without saying good-bye. We came fast as we could. Howdy, Milo, Mr. Tagg." She stepped into the dusky cabin, put the basket on the table, and pulled off the cloth. It was full of muffins as round and big as a man's fist.

When Jimmy stood up to greet her, he saw a small face peek around her skirt. "Ingabumbee!" he cried. "Come here, come to Jimmy."

The little boy toddled forward, one chubby hand still clinging to Mrs. Roberts's skirt. His red hair was fluffy, his cheeks rosy plump. He wore a long-sleeved gingham smock that almost covered his tiny bare feet. When Jimmy swooped him up, his wet diaper soaked the front of Jimmy's shirt.

"I am glad to see you, 'Bumbee, and I'm going to tell Old Mother all about you." Jimmy didn't complain about the diaper or mention that he had long ago hoped Ingabumbee could ride north with him. It mattered more to Jimmy that the child was happy with the Robertses. So far no relatives had come forward.

"My Lucy's with Tom and the fellas," said Mrs. Roberts. "Both her and 'Bumbee started walkin' a couple weeks ago and they are into everything, messy as two chipmunks. We can't stay. As it is, we'll have to camp at Diamond Springs again. I sure am gonna miss you, Jim." She crushed him to her with a hug stronger than Milo's. Jimmy would always remember how good Mrs. Roberts smelled, of fresh sunshine and sweat.

At one o'clock that afternoon Jimmy and Pen rode out of Ruby Valley. Farewells were quick. Milo had helped Jimmy into the stirrups, then from inside his shirt he took out the small Bible Jimmy had left on the hearth.

"You forgot to pack this, son."

"Didn't forget," Jimmy said. "I just don't need it. There's never time to read anyhow."

Milo smiled up at Jimmy, then patted him affectionately on the arm. "Well now, Jim, that's where I disagree with you." He tucked the Scriptures into Jimmy's saddlebag, slapped the horse's rump, then lifted his arm in a farewell wave as the animals broke into a gallop.

Milo and Mr. Tagg gave each other a sad smile, then they watched the northward trail. Soft white dust followed the boys long after they were out of sight.

23

THE HIDEOUT

Jimmy and Pen reached the northern end of the Ruby Mountain Range an hour before sunset. Shadowy canyons met the foothills, which were bushy with juniper and sage. Beyond was the desert, purple and brown in the waning light. They were far from the Overland Trail.

While the horses drank from a wide, shallow stream, Jimmy gathered twigs and leaves for the fire. He opened up a small leather pouch that had been smoked in beef fat to make it waterproof. Inside were the matches Mr. Tagg had made for them, short pieces of waxed cord dipped in sulphur. When rubbed against a rough stone, the tip ignited. It had the horrible smell of rotten eggs, but its blue flame quickly blazed through the kindling.

Jimmy was glad Pen was with him — for the companionship and so he could hunt the small game they would need for food. Jimmy's head ached so much at the end of a day he just wanted to lie down and sleep. Milo had been right. He was not well enough to travel alone.

Suddenly Pen appeared, running through the brush, the rifle swinging at his side. He was gesturing frantically and not until he reached Jimmy did he speak.

"Quick, Jimmy," he said, kicking dirt onto the flames, "put out the fire."

Jimmy hurriedly scooped sand into the pit. "Why? What is it?" he asked.

But Pen only motioned with his head. Together they untethered their horses and led them to a stand of cottonwoods on the other side of the stream. The bedrolls and gear were still tied to the saddles.

"Jimmy," he said in a low voice, "I heard men below the ridge there, drunken men. They were talking about a *murder*. Their horses are corraled in that box canyon we passed. What should we do?"

Jimmy stubbed at the ground with the toe of his boot. His head hurt and he was hungry. Soon it would be dark and they would need to eat. But the idea of spying on outlaws appealed to him more.

"Let's go see," Jimmy whispered.

With a nod, Pen slung the rifle over his shoulder. He led them into the stream where the sound of water would muffle their running. They followed it up to the south fork where white water flowed too swiftly for them to wade. Trailing its narrow beach they soon came to a fallen log that lay across the river, inches above the rapids. It was slippery with moss. With spray misting their arms and legs, the boys carefully crept along its trunk, through its tangle of roots, then onto shore.

Pen pointed to a thicket beyond the trees. When they reached it, they flattened themselves, face-down in a spongy bed of pine needles. Jimmy's feet squished uncomfortably in his boots as he crawled with Pen toward a ledge. From their bellies they looked below.

Eight men lounged around a campfire, all rough-looking characters, laughing loudly. A brown jug rolled in the dirt on its side, first kicked by one muddy boot, then another. Its missing cork indicated to Jimmy that whatever liquid had been inside, was no longer.

His eyes widened when he noticed the dapper gentleman off to the side. The man looked familiar. He was cleaning a gun and laughing along with the others. When he turned slightly, revealing a handsome profile, Jimmy knew who it was.

Jack Slade.

So Milo and Mr. Tagg had been right. Jack Slade wasn't to be trusted. Maybe he *had* killed twenty-two people. Jimmy strained to see if there were any grisly mementos lying about, but saw only sacks of U.S. Mail and an assortment of luggage and small chests.

And he was in with the Rex Dooley gang! Jimmy began crawling backward, away from the ledge, pulling at Pen's soggy jeans so he would do the same. Another time, another day, Jimmy would have attempted a daring rescue of the mail. He would have stampeded their horses. He would have rounded up a posse to hunt down the thieves. A little danger would be exciting.

But today Jimmy wanted no trouble. He was wearing his eagle feather. Old Mother was waiting for him and he was not going to break a promise.

Moments before sunset, the boys made it back to the grove of cottonwoods. Without needing to speak, they pulled themselves into their saddles and rode out. A full moon was climbing skyward and, like a trusted old friend, it would help the boys see their way to safety.

24

BUFFALO

In the days that followed, the boys rode north along the outskirts of the lush Cache Valley in Utah Territory. Jimmy wanted to avoid the Mormon settlements. He did not want anyone to interrupt his journey with questions or offers of hospitality.

When they came to a rise and saw in the distance a shimmery thread of water, Jimmy became excited. This was *Piupa*, the Snake River, where he had first fished and swum with his Indian family. He and Pen had reached the Territory that Congress would soon name Idaho.

"There's Fort Hall," he said, pointing to the stockades in the grassy bottomland. Shoshoni traded here, which meant Jimmy might see old friends. Because the fort was on the Oregon Trail it would also be bustling with travelers who stopped to rest and repair wagons. But as the boys came closer, they realized there was no smoke rising from the five chimneys and only a tattered rag dangled from the flagpole. The post was abandoned.

They rode through the empty yard to a bluff. Looking down, they found a steep trail to the river. While their horses drank, Jimmy and Pen took off their boots and trousers, unbuttoned their shirts, then raced each other in. The cold water felt good. Jimmy rolled onto his back and, as he did, he felt something brush his arm. A large speckled trout quickly twitched away from him, then swam to the middle of the current. This gave Jimmy an idea.

"Pen," he said in a quiet voice, "better build us a fire because I intend to catch us some dinner."

Jimmy let himself drift out to deeper water, facedown, his legs and arms floating like driftwood. Ever so slowly he turned his head to the side to take a breath. The water was crystal clear and he could see the trout's rainbowed tail finning back and forth.

Before the fish could blink, Jimmy's hand had glided under its belly, his fingers hooked the gills, and in one swift movement he tossed it to the bank. It landed flopping by Pen's muddy feet. Pen was so startled he dropped his shirt in the sand.

"Lordy Jim, I'm glad as heck you weren't catchin' us a bear for dinner."

* * *

For two days the boys continued north along *Piupa*, stopping often to water the horses and to let Jimmy rest under a shady tree. Though his wound had healed, he was bothered by headaches.

When the river turned east, Jimmy's heart quickened. He had camped here with Washakie. It was from that rock he had launched himself into a beautiful dive because Nahanee was watching and Jimmy had wanted to show off. Instead, he had landed such a slap on his belly, even now he cringed to remember his embarrassment.

The Teton Valley spread before them, gray-blue with sage and, in the far distance, the snowy western peaks of the Tetons. The beauty filled Jimmy with happiness. How wonderful those days were, when he was Dawii, Young Brother to the chief. The land was still lovely and it was alive. Sage grouse fluttered among the brush, and a family of pronghorn antelope scattered away from the trail, leaping as they ran. Overhead came the cry of a red-tailed hawk. Wind moved clouds across the sky as if pulling cotton; it stirred the tall grass.

Along the riverbank walked three big black birds, twice as large as crows. They looked like bullies, hunched over and serious, as they searched for seeds and bugs. Jimmy laughed out loud, pointing to them.

"You watch, Pen, soon those ravens will find a dead fish that floats ashore. Indians call them *The bird that never goes hungry*. They'll eat me and you if we sit still long enough. Come on!"

They rode to the top of a grassy knoll, then galloped downhill for the fun of it. In the shade of an aspen they saw a light brown buffalo calf. Its mother was nearby, grazing on wheat grass. Her coat was dark brown with tufts of shedding fur.

"*Bojono,*" Jimmy whispered, remembering when Old Mother had taught him the word. *Buffalo.* Shoshoni followed the herds and lived well because of them. This meant his Indian family was closer than he'd realized. He wanted to hurry.

With each mile, more and more *bojono* dotted the landscape. Some would lift their huge furry heads to watch the two strangers on horseback. The boys rode for another hour, finally splashing through a shallow stream as they reached the crest of a hill. In the valley below was a sight that made Jimmy's heart swell with emotion.

Dozens of cone-shaped tipis were clustered near the river. Its sandy beach was noisy with children playing. Women worked over stretched-out hides and there was smoke from cooking fires. Men gathered in circles, possibly hunters and elders. A drumbeat came on the wind. On the other side of the river, a herd of spotted ponies moved among the grass.

Jimmy tried to take everything in. There was something so beautiful, something so deeply familiar, he knew this was a Shoshoni camp. But for a moment he felt sick. What if he was too late to see Old Mother alive? Would Nahanee be here? What about Nampa and Ga-mu, Poog and the others? Would they be angry he'd been away so long?

At the sight of so many Indians, Pen began to

shake. He touched Jimmy's sleeve. "We're out-numbered, Jim. Maybe I should turn back, maybe this wasn't such a good idea me comin' with you. Maybe they'll wanna scalp a white boy like me."

Jimmy smiled at his friend. Without explaining, he picked up the reins and clicked his tongue. His horse headed downhill, and in a dignified trot carried Jimmy toward the village.

25

WASHAKIE

A pack of barking dogs swarmed out to the meadow to meet Pen and Jimmy. This made Jimmy laugh. He remembered fondly how there were always dogs around camp; some were pets, but most were strays who made a lot of noise and dust when visitors came.

Three young boys on pintos galloped out, their braids flying and their small bare chests puffed up as if they were warriors. *"Yes, it is Dawii,"* one shouted as they circled the pair, then formed ranks. Proudly they escorted the newcomers into camp. Now Jimmy was certain his family was here; even these boys expected him.

As they crossed the meadow toward the tipis, Jimmy's heart beat fast. He was thrilled to see so many familiar faces in the crowd gathering around them. Children raced each other between the lodges to be first to get a good look. Someone called Jimmy's name, then someone else. An older woman he didn't recognize walked alongside his horse with her hand on his knee. She smiled up at him.

Pen, however, had never met an Indian, and now there were hundreds, all staring and wondering about him. He was so nervous, color had drained from his face. His stomach churned as if it might empty itself on the spot.

"Jimmy," he said. "I'm not feeling s'good." Even though Pen's words were not Shoshoni, the old woman seemed to understand. She came to his side and touched his hand. He let her help him from his saddle.

As several women guided Pen to a shady tree, Jimmy saw movement in the crowd to his right. He knew immediately that the tall man stepping out was Washakie. His war bonnet of eagle feathers looked like a high white crown, and his hair hung loose over his shoulders. He wore a shirt of blue cotton with a buckskin vest, beaded down the front.

"Dawii . . ." he said, motioning for someone to take Jimmy's horse. But the chief was too overcome with emotion to continue. His arms enfolded Jimmy with the affection he reserved for his family.

They walked along the river. It was late afternoon and sunlight glimmered off the water where tiny flies and mosquitos hovered. A fish broke the surface to feed, then with a small splash of its tail, swam down to the sandy bottom. For a long time Jimmy and Washakie sat cross-legged in the grass. Neither spoke.

After so many hours on horseback Jimmy's head hurt, but he didn't want to sleep, not yet. He drank in every familiar sight and sound. How good it was to hear children playing again, to hear the voices of women working together. Somewhere in the distance a man sang to a slow beat of a drum. Wood smoke drifted in the warm breeze, bringing with it the delicious aroma of roasting meat.

Jimmy glanced at Washakie's profile. He was still a handsome man. The deep scar under his left cheekbone was from an arrow long ago, a scar like Jimmy now had. Did he suffer from headaches, too? There was so much Jimmy wanted to ask his brother, so much he wanted to tell him.

For now though, they would enjoy each other's quiet company. Washakie would take him to see Old Mother when the time was right. Jimmy closed his eyes to savor the thought that had just come to him.

I am home. Finally, I am home.

26

A GENTLE SCOLDING

When the afternoon sun dipped below the tree-tops, long shadows spilled across the river. Washakie turned toward Jimmy.

"It is good you are here, Dawii. Our dear Old Mother asks for you and now I can tell her, *'Yes, Dawii has returned to us.'*"

He pointed to the wedge-shaped scar above Jimmy's eye and grinned. "But watch out, Old Mother will scold you for that."

After sunset Washakie took Jimmy to a tipi in the center of camp. He scratched on the outside. When a voice answered, he opened the flap, then ducked inside the oval doorway, motioning for Jimmy to follow.

It was dark except for a small fire in the center. Jimmy could see the shapes of three people sitting at the back of the lodge. One of them placed some dried buffalo droppings on the coals, then poked them until they blazed into a warm, smokeless fire. Yellow light swept up the sides of the tent.

Jimmy was overjoyed to see Old Mother. She sat between two of her daughters, staring toward him. Her unseeing eyes were milky white. She held out her arms for Jimmy, listening as he stepped around the fire to her. Tears of happiness rolled down her cheeks. She tried to talk, but her crying made her mouth shake and no words came.

"Old Mother," Jimmy said, coming to his knees to hug her. She was smaller than he'd remembered, but the tenderness in her embrace was the same. She held his face in her hands, as if to see him by touch. Her fingers felt his wet cheeks. She caressed his hair, his forehead, but when she discovered the smooth welt above his eye, she frowned.

"What has happened to my little son?"

"I met an Indian in the dark, Old Mother. He didn't like me."

"Aii! I knew there was trouble. In two more sleeps, if you had not come, Nampa and others were going to search for you. I knew you were hurt." She waved her hand as if to dismiss the thought, then leaned into her backrest. The excitement of the moment had exhausted her.

"Tell me about your family," she whispered.

"They know I've come to see you, Old Mother. I have a gift." Jimmy reached into his pocket and took out a blue silk scarf. Placing it in her hands he said, "My mother wants you to have this. She gave it to me when I left the Great Salt Lake City."

More tears filled the old woman's eyes, but she was smiling. Her fingers rubbed the fine silk. "Dawii," she said softly, "this is a happy day."

"Yes, Old Mother, it is."

27

JIMMY'S SEARCH

Two grandmothers set up a tipi for Jimmy and Pen on a raised bank near the river. They positioned it on the northeast side of a cottonwood tree so it would have sunshine in the morning, then shade in the afternoon when the day became hot.

The cover was made from moose hide and, when wrapped around the nine poles, looked like a short brown cone. The hem stopped two inches above ground, but a liner on the inside would keep out drafts and moisture.

Around the fire the women arranged two backrests, some cooking utensils, and a pile of kindling. Pen ran his hands over the thick dark fur of the buffalo robe that was to be his bed. He was fascinated how sunlight made the curved walls look golden and how, high overhead, the crisscross of poles formed a beautiful design. Blue sky showed through the opening.

"I declare, Jim, this beats that gloomy old cabin any day." Pen had recovered from his fright of the day before. The old woman named Singing Grass had cared for him as if he were her son; Pen-the-orphan was an orphan no more. On his feet was a new pair of moccasins, and he wore a long shirt made from soft deerskin. It was fringed at the knees and along the shoulders and sleeves.

"You look good," Jimmy told him. "Made you take a bath, didn't they?"

Pen laughed. His dark blond hair looked several shades lighter and gone were the bits of leaves and twigs that had nested in his curls. "Alls I could think of," he said, "was long ago when I was real, real little. A lady from the wagon train carried me into a river, then afterward dressed me in a big clean shirt of her husband's. It felt so good I wished she could have been my mother. That's what yesterday's bath made me remember."

Jimmy looked at his friend. "I'm glad you came with me, Pen. I wouldn't have made it all this way without you."

Every afternoon Old Mother's friends helped her walk to the riverbank where it was cool. Dappled sunlight filtered down through the cottonwoods where they sat listening to their grandchildren play. When Old Mother heard Jimmy approach, her face lifted with a smile.

"Dawii. I am ready to hear more from your book." She patted the ground next to her, inviting him to sit. Ever since she learned Jimmy had a Bible with words from *Bea Oppah*, the Great Spirit, she insisted he read and translate for her.

"Yes, Old Mother, I'll read. But first I must ask you something." Here Jimmy hesitated. He wished she understood English so he could talk without the others hearing. Instead, he leaned close and spoke in her ear.

"Old Mother," he said, "since I came eight suns ago, I have looked through camp and beyond. I have not seen Nahanee or her family."

Old Mother nodded. "Nor have I seen her." She laughed at her joke, then stopped herself. Dawii was speaking from his heart; this was not the time to tease.

"Many have gone to the river north of here," she offered, "to welcome back the Leaping Fish with a blessing ceremony. Washakie is there."

Jimmy knew Old Mother was talking about the chinook salmon and their annual return from the ocean. The ceremony was sacred, with hours of prayer and thanksgiving. Like the buffalo, salmon were respected and honored because year after year they sustained the people.

"Before the snows," Old Mother continued, "Nahanee was here. She and her mother made moccasins for me. We talked about the bear and we talked about you."

Jimmy's heart leapt. Nahanee hadn't forgotten

him after all. "What did she say about me?" he asked.

Old Mother listened to the river for several moments before answering. "There are many things on a young woman's heart when each moon passes."

What did Old Mother mean? Was Nahanee in love with someone? Jimmy was afraid to ask, because he was afraid of what the answer might be. He remembered something from long ago. It was the evening after he had rescued Nahanee from the grizzly bear. By the fire in Washakie's tipi her grateful parents promised him a gift: Their daughter Nahanee would one day be his bride.

But Jimmy had said no. *I do not want a wife.* Those words now haunted him.

"Old Mother," he said. "I am going to go north to welcome the Leaping Fish. When I return, you and I will have much to talk about."

"Yes, son, I know."

28

BIG FISH GIRL

The next day Pen and Jimmy saddled their horses and set out with three others: Mozo the elder, Nampa, and Ga-mu, old friends of Jimmy's. They rode north toward the river that white men would one day name the Salmon.

The timbered hills were lush from melting snow. Waterfalls could be heard, a high whisper in the clear air. Everywhere, Jimmy recognized landmarks. *I am home*, he wanted to shout.

The river twisted through canyons. Bighorn sheep blended into the hillsides so perfectly that only when they leapt from rock to rock could Jimmy see the animals. After two days of travel there was a wide pebbled beach and, in the middle of the river, a sandbar where four tipis were camped.

"We'll rest here," Mozo said. He dismounted carefully, as if his legs were stiff. His silver braids were wrapped halfway down with otter fur and there were two eagle feathers at his temple. Jimmy felt deep admiration for Mozo. He took the reins of his horse, then helped Ga-mu turn the others to pasture.

In the narrow part of the stream, a large boulder formed a bridge, making it easy to cross over to the island without getting moccasins wet. A woman with a cradleboard on her back greeted the travelers, then called to someone inside her lodge. Out stepped an attractive girl about Jimmy's age. She was quite round with a plump face, a familiar face.

It was Big Fish Girl and Jimmy was not glad to see her. Not only was she bossy, she weighed at least eighty pounds more than he did, which meant she could wrestle him down in a wink. Many times they had quarreled. Once he called her a bad name and she had shoved him into a marsh and snapped his hunting bow in half. Jimmy eventually decided to be nice to her. He knew it would be safer to wrestle a grizzly than to make Big Fish Girl mad again.

"Hello, Dawii," she smiled. "I see you found me." She turned away and began walking toward the far end of the campsite. Since Nampa and the others were talking, Jimmy followed Big Fish Girl. They sat down on the tip of the sandbar where the river flowed past them on both sides, as if they were in the bow of a canoe.

She turned her brown eyes on him. "I've waited a long time for you," she said. Her boldness embarrassed Jimmy. He glanced back at the four tipis, hoping to see Nahanee or her mother.

After an awkward silence he finally spoke. "Mozo is taking us to the Blessing Ceremony. I want to see old friends."

Big Fish Girl's face darkened. "If you're looking for Nahanee, you are too late."

Jimmy glared at her. "What are you saying?" he asked. His heart was beating fast and he felt a tightness in his throat.

"I am saying that you are eight moons too late. Nahanee has a husband. She is big with child. But I, who waited patiently, am not married. My lodge is yours, Dawii. I will make you very warm when the snows come."

But Jimmy wasn't listening. He felt dizzy and suddenly his head hurt so much he wanted to lie down. If only he could sleep, he might have the courage to turn back.

This wasn't his home after all. He hated it here. He hated the smiling round face of Big Fish Girl.

29

THE NECKLACE

Pen noticed Jimmy with the horses. "Jim!" he called, running across the field. "Where're you going?"

Jimmy stroked the muscular neck of his pinto. His eyes were sad. "I'm going back," he said. "I'll wait with Old Mother until you and the others return, then we'll ride together to Salt Lake City."

"But why? Why are you leaving? I don't understand. Was that girl the one you're looking for, is she Nahanee?"

"*Her?* No. That's Big Fish Girl. She thinks she owns the world. Every time I see her I have bad dreams."

Pen threw his hands up in frustration. "You're leaving because of her? She's just a girl."

114

Jimmy closed his eyes and lay his head on the horse's silky mane. He was heartbroken that Nahanee had married. If only he'd realized she meant so much to him, he never would have stayed away so long.

Wanting to comfort him, Pen touched Jimmy's shoulder. He didn't know what to say.

"I should have come sooner," Jimmy said miserably.

A voice distracted them. They looked up to see Mozo walking slowly toward them. The elder's arm was raised as if to say *don't go*.

When Jimmy explained why he wanted to leave, Mozo was quiet. Finally he nodded as if he understood. "I cannot tell you what to do, Dawii. But I can tell you it is not good to hide when the heart is sad. Come to the Blessing Ceremony. You will learn there is much to be thankful for, even when you're unhappy. That is all I have to say."

Mozo walked back to the sandbar where there was smoke from two campfires. The good smell of fish roasting made Jimmy hungry. He thought about Old Mother and remembered how she once scolded him for disobeying Mozo.

Have you lived so long that you know more than your elders? is what she'd said.

Because Jimmy hadn't listened to Mozo, he ended up lost in the woods, alone. He did not want to make another mistake like that and he did not want to be like Mr. Lantern, a man who thought his way was the only way.

Jimmy looked at Pen and tried to smile. "I've changed my mind," he said. "Let's join the others."

The next day, they continued north. Jimmy counted nineteen tipis near the river. There were dogs and children and cooking fires; there were boys on ponies racing each other below a hillside. Some of them cantered over to escort the travelers into camp. Jimmy didn't feel the excitement he'd felt two weeks earlier. His heart was heavy thinking about Nahanee. He slid off his horse and handed the reins to a boy eager to help.

Pen was surrounded by children who'd never before seen such yellow hair or freckled skin. He was not nervous this time; instead he was friendly. Pen was enjoying his new status as Friend of Dawii, Son of Singing Grass.

A group of mothers and daughters watched Jimmy fondly. When he saw Nahanee among them his heart fell, but then it soared with happiness.

She stood in front of her lodge, her eyes cast down to show respect. She was more beautiful than Jimmy had remembered and when she lifted her head to smile at him he thought he would burst with joy.

Big Fish Girl had lied. Nahanee was not big with child. Her soft deerskin dress fell gracefully over her slim figure. Around her neck was the magnificent bear claw necklace Jimmy had given her five years ago.

Nahanee had waited for Dawii to return and she was wearing his necklace to say so.

30

THE BLESSING

Jimmy and Nahanee wandered along a creek where fragrant white flowers of the syringa bloomed. In the shady woods there were violets, blue and yellow, and ferns. As they talked, Jimmy was aware of the aroma of balsam and pine, and the pleasant twittering of birds. Never had he known a more beautiful day or a happier moment, but he did know this: He loved Nahanee with all his heart.

When they stopped by a small waterfall, he found himself gently pulling her to him. He breathed in the wonderful scent of her hair and skin. They glanced at each other, then laughed at their shyness. Jimmy wanted to kiss her, but he wasn't sure how to go about it.

"Nahanee," he said, holding her hands in his. He gazed at her lovely face and felt lost for words. "I . . . I . . . want to marry you, Nahanee."

She looked into his eyes. "I will be your woman, Dawii."

Jimmy let out a huge sigh of relief, then threw his head back in laughter. No longer shy, he swept her into a hug. With one hand under her head and an arm around her waist, he kissed her.

Nahanee was going to be his wife. Wild with joy, he kissed her again.

Later that afternoon Jimmy found Pen by the river with Mozo, who was showing him how to string a bow. There was something about Jimmy's manner that made them both stop and look at him.

"Big Fish Girl lied, didn't she?" asked Pen.

Jimmy laughed. "Yes." He picked up a small, flat stone and threw it low so that it skipped several times across the water. He picked up another stone. This one he rolled between his fingers, thinking.

"Nahanee and I will marry before the snows," he said. "Pen, I won't be returning to Salt Lake, at least not for a while."

Jimmy translated for his elder. A light breeze moved the ends of Mozo's gray hair, which hung loose down his back. He grinned. "You will be warmer than most of us, Dawii. This is good that you have come back to us."

"Yes, Mozo, I am glad to be home." In English, Jimmy said, "Pen, if you don't mind wintering here, I will ride back with you in the spring, then my family will be able to meet my wife. What we'll do then, I'm not sure."

Pen's eyes widened and he gave Jimmy's shoulder a hearty shake. "Count me in. I wouldn't miss that for anything."

Before dawn the next morning families began to gather in a clearing by the river, forming a semicircle. The air was cold. Some mothers had babies in cradleboards, others left their smaller children sleeping in the lodges.

The Blessing Ceremony began the moment the first rays of sunlight split through the trees. Washakie and Mozo stood near the fire where the fragrance of cedar and sweet sage rose with the smoke. They held fans made of eagle feathers, which they waved through the incense. A slow drumbeat marked time.

Jimmy and Nahanee walked with the others past the fire, praying silently, then sipping from a gourd of river water. Pen followed with his new friends, Nampa and Ga-mu. Mozo raised his arms to the sky and began to sing:

"*Bea Oppah*, grant the Leaping Fish a safe return . . . *Bea Oppah*, grant us peace . . ."

Jimmy looked at Nahanee. Sunlight lay on her cheek, her eyes were closed with reverence. How good she was. How he loved her.

As the hour passed, Jimmy began to feel a deep peace. Mozo was right, there was always something to be thankful for. He thought about his family in Salt Lake and about his friends Will and Nick Cone, Mr. Tagg and Milo, little Ingabumbee.

"*Bea Oppah*, take care of them all," Jimmy sang. "*Bea Oppah*, help me be a good husband." He took Nahanee's hand, then raised his face to the sun.

AFTERWORD

Jimmy Spoon and the Pony Express is a blend of history and fiction. For example, Billy (William F. "Buffalo Bill") Cody was one of the youngest riders at age fourteen, but his route was actually east of Utah.

Joseph Alfred ("Captain Jack") Slade rode between Fort Laramie and Horseshoe Station in Wyoming. He was one of the more notorious riders, a whiskey guzzler and desperado who boasted of twenty-six murders. Eventually he was hanged by vigilantes in Virginia City, Montana.

Twenty-three-year-old James Butler ("Wild Bill") Hickok was not a Pony Express rider, but he was a stable hand at the Rock Creek Station near the Kansas-Nebraska state line. It was there by the

Little Blue River that on the hot, dusty day of July 12, 1861, he killed several members of the Mc-Canles gang. Accounts vary, but one legend says that David McCanles enjoyed making fun of Hickok's protruding upper lip by calling him "Duck Bill." This teasing may or may not have led up to the murder. As a result, "Duck Bill" became "Wild Bill," a gunslinger and U.S. Marshal of Abilene, Kansas. It is said, however, that he spent much of his time at the poker table.

During the summer of 1861, brothers Samuel and Orion Clemens traveled by stagecoach from Missouri to Carson City, thrilling to the sight of a Pony Express rider. Because of the heat — and because there were no female passengers — they rode much of the way in their Skivvies. Orion became assistant to Governor James W. Nye of the newly formed Nevada Territory. For some time Sam was Orion's assistant, then he took a job reporting for the Virginia City *Territorial Enterprise*, writing under the name of Mark Twain. He describes these adventures and his meetings with Brigham Young and Jack Slade in *Roughing It*, published in 1872.

Historians disagree about the exact numbers and locations of Pony Express Stations in Nevada. A few stone foundations and crumbling adobe walls exist, but most remnants are gone. Exceptions are Fort Churchill, which is now a state monument, and the blacksmith shop at Friday's Station. Some of the original log cabin from Ruby Valley Station was moved and reconstructed; it is now displayed at the Northeastern Nevada Museum in Elko.

Alexander Majors did issue each boy a Holy Bible, believing their spiritual health was as important as their physical health. *Jimmy Spoon* is not the complete story of the Pony Express, nor does it begin to tell about the many heroes and colorful events. Some of the fine books listed in the bibliography do that.

GLOSSARY

[*Sho.*: Shoshoni, *Sp.*: Spanish]

alkali — salty, fine dirt found in deserts where a lake or pond has evaporated

Bea Oppah — [*Sho.*]; Great Father, Great Spirit, God

Bannock — "hair in backward motion," referring to men's pompadour, Idaho tribe

bojono — [*Sho.*]; buffalo

Conestoga — a covered wagon used by pioneers; named after Conestoga Valley, Pennsylvania, where the wagons were built

Confederates — soldiers from the league of Southern States that seceded from the United States in 1860–61 (Alabama, Arkansas, Florida, Georgia, Louisiana, Mississippi, North Carolina, South Carolina, Tennessee, Texas, and Virginia)

Dawii — [*Sho.*]; young brother

Ga-mu — [*Sho.*]; rabbit

Gosiute — "dust people," a Shoshoni-speaking tribe from the southwest area of Utah's Great Salt Lake and parts of Nevada

Ingabumbee — [*Sho.*]; red hair

mestengo — [*Sp.*]; wild (mustang horse)

mochila — [*Sp.*]; knapsack (the leather rectangle with four mail pouches that fits over the pommel and cantle of the Pony Express rider's saddle; total weight was less than thirteen pounds, or one third of an ordinary western saddle)

Mozo — [*Sho.*]; whisker

Nampa — [*Sho.*]; moccasin

Paiute — "Ute of the water," Nevada tribe

Piupa — [*Sho.*]; Snake River

Skivvies — a man's short-sleeved undershirt/underwear

Tosa-ibi — [*Sho.*]; Soda Springs, Idaho

transcontinental telegraph — the coast-to-coast planting of telegraph poles that finally met in Salt Lake City, Utah, on October 24, 1861

tybo — [*Sho.*]; white person

Washakie — [*Sho.*]; rawhide rattle

BIBLIOGRAPHY

Bloss, Roy S. *Pony Express, The Great Gamble.* Berkeley, CA: Howell-North, 1959.

Bowman, John S., gen. ed. *The World Almanac of the American West.* New York: World Almanac, 1986.

Bradley, Glenn D. *The Story of the Pony Express.* Chicago: A. C. McClurg & Co., 1913.

Capps, Benjamin. *The Great Chiefs.* Alexandria, VA: Time-Life Books, 1975.

Chapman, Arthur. *The Pony Express.* New York: Putnam's, 1932.

Cody, William F. *The Life and Adventures of "Buffalo Bill," an Autobiography.* Clinton, MA: The Colonial Press, 1927.

Corporation of the President of The Church of Jesus Christ of Latter-day Saints. *The Beehive House.* Salt Lake City, UT: 1978.

Curran, Harold. *Fearful Crossing: The Central Overland Trail Through Nevada.* Las Vegas: Nevada Publishers, 1982.

Deseret News. Salt Lake City, UT: 1850–1860.

Grun, Bernard. *The Timetables of History.* New York: Simon & Schuster, 1982.

Jensen, Lee. *The Pony Express.* New York: Grosset & Dunlap, 1955.

Bibliography

Lennon, Nigey. *The Sagebrush Bohemian: Mark Twain in California.* New York: Paragon House, 1990.

Madsen, Brigham D. *The Shoshoni Frontier and the Bear River Massacre.* Salt Lake City: University of Utah Press, 1985.

Nevada Bureau of Land Management. *The Pony Express in Nevada.* Lake Tahoe, NV: 1976.

Nevin, David. *The Expressmen.* New York: Time-Life Books, 1974.

Patent, Dorothy Hinshaw; photographs by William Munoz. *Where the Wild Horses Roam.* New York: Clarion Books, 1989.

Perry, John, and Jane Greverus Perry. *The Sierra Club Guide to the Natural Areas of New Mexico, Arizona and Nevada.* San Francisco: Sierra Club Books, 1985.

Reinfeld, Fred. *Pony Express.* New York: Macmillan, 1966.

Robertson, James I., Jr. *Civil War! America Becomes One Nation.* New York: Knopf, 1992.

Root, Frank A. *The Overland Stage to California.* Topeka, KS: W.Y. Morgan, 1901.

Seymour, John. *The Forgotten Household Crafts.* New York: Knopf, 1987.

Sho-Ban News. Fort Hall, ID: 1987–1992.

Spencer, Clarissa Young, with Mabel Harmer. *Brigham Young At Home.* Salt Lake City: Schocken Books, 1982.

Stein, R. Conrad. *The Story of the Pony Express.* Chicago: Children's Press, 1981.

Stevenson, Augusta. *Buffalo Bill, Boy of the Plains.*

New York: Bobbs-Merrill, 1948.

Storer, Tracy I., and Robert L. Usinger. *Sierra Nevada Natural History*. Berkeley: University of California Press, 1963.

Twain, Mark. *Roughing It*. Hartford, CT: American Publishing Co., 1872; New York: New American Library, 1962.

Visscher, William Lightfoot. *The Pony Express*. Chicago: The Charles T. Powner Co., 1908, 1946.

Waldman, Carl; maps and illustrations by Molly Brown. *Atlas of the North American Indian*. New York: Facts on File Publications, 1985.

Wheeler, Sessions S. *The Nevada Desert*. Caldwell, ID: Caxton Printers, Ltd., 1989.

Williamson, Darcy, and Steven Shephard. *Salmon River Legends and Campfire Cuisine*. Bend, OR: Maverick Publications, 1988.

Wilson, Elijah Nicholas. *Among the Shoshones*. Medford, OR: Pine Cone Publishers, 1910.

ABOUT THE AUTHOR

Kristiana Gregory is a noted author of historical fiction for young readers. Her books have been nominated for numerous state awards, and her first novel, *Jenny of the Tetons*, won the 1989 Golden Kite Award for fiction. Her most recent novel, *Earthquake at Dawn*, was an ALA Best Book for Young Adults.

    Ms. Gregory lives in California with her family.

ALSO BY
KRISTIANA GREGORY

Jenny of the Tetons
The Legend of Jimmy Spoon
Earthquake at Dawn

8/97 Follett #12.00

Fic/Gre

Gregory, Kristiana

JIMMY SPOON AND THE PONY EXPRESS